SIX WHITE HORSES
THE COMPLETE ADVENTURES
OF THE GADGET MAN, VOLUME 3

SIX WHITE HORSES

THE COMPLETE ADVENTURES OF THE GADGET MAN, VOLUME 3

LESTER DENT

PRIMARY ILLUSTRATORS:
ALBERT MICALE
PAUL ORBAN

ALTUS

PRESS

ALTUS PRESS

2023

TABLE OF CONTENTS

INTRODUCTION

BOTH THE SHADOW'S creator Walter B. Gibson and his editor, John L. Nanovic, claimed to have conceived the idea that ultimately led to the creation of *Crime Busters,* and indirectly Lester Dent's Gadget Man series.

Street and Smith was searching for a new type of magazine, one that would showcase a strong hero, like *The Shadow* or *Doc Savage*. But in the Roosevelt Recession of 1937-38, new titles were a risky venture.

Gibson's idea was a "seed" magazine featuring three new heroes by top S&S writers. If any one grew popular, his thinking went, that character could be spun off into his own title and replaced by a new candidate.

> "I was talking to [S&S Business Manager Henry] Ralston about more character magazines," Gibson explained. "And I was thinking myself of a magician detective, though I didn't know how it would go. He said, 'Well, it's costly to start a character magazine, and if it flops....' So I suggested that they put out one with three characters in it. And then whichever one went well, that would be it. They went ahead, but they put in five or six characters. Everyone else used his own name, even Lester Dent with his Bufa stories, but they asked me if I would put on the 'Maxwell Grant' because then

they would advertise it in the Shadow magazine—'Get the stories by Maxwell Grant'—so it was really a favor to them on my part."

Nanovic recalled it this way:

"That was mostly my idea," he said. "And I don't want to brag about it because it didn't do too well. It just got along. Here we had a stable of famous writers. Gibson. Robeson. All of them were selling pretty well. So I said, 'The guys who like these fellas should like them in other magazines.' So we made up *Crime Busters*. These were all lead house names. We had like ten in every issue."

Henry W. Ralston and editor Nanovic ultimately decided to run more, shorter tales in what they dubbed *Crime Busters*. Gibson already had a character in mind, a traveling magician-sleuth named Norgil, which he wrote under the house name of Maxwell Grant. Ted Tinsley was contacted and created Carrie Cashin, a strong female detective. He did this under his own name.

No doubt Lester Dent was high on the list of writers S&S recruited for *Crime Busters*. His Doc Savage novels had been popular for four years. No doubt also, S&S attempted to prevail upon Dent to write the new series under the Kenneth Robeson house name. There is no doubt Dent resisted strenuously. He hated the Robeson byline, was initially surprised when the name was attached to his early Doc novels. Dent stood firm. He would contribute to the new magazine as Dent, or not at all.

Dent was a formula writer. He also loved gadgets. And by 1937 had developed a kind of screwball humor approach to Doc Savage.

From the little we know about it, a lot can be inferred about the genesis of Click Rush, the Gadget Man.

Sometime in 1936 but no later than June, 1937, Lester Dent rolled a carbon-paper sandwich into his Remington typewriter and rattled off the following:

TALKING DOG

The block of stone was about five feet long, two feet wide, and a foot thick. It was granite. It probably weighed over a ton.

It fell fifteen stories and missed John Magic by the length of an arm.

There was a crash. A hole burst open in the sidewalk, dust puffed and pieces of rock flew about, and across the street a man let out a yell. Or bleat.

Whether Dent changed his mind in mid-stride, or kept writing is unknown. Only this variant first page survived among his manuscripts.

During Dent's 1936 sabbatical from writing Doc Savage, he cracked several prestigious markets, including *Argosy* and *Black Mask*. He tried but failed to break into *Detective Fiction Weekly*. There is an excellent chance that the unpublished "Talking Dog" was a *DFW* reject that Dent dusted off when the *Crime Busters* opportunity arose.

It's possible Dent took the first adventure featuring John Magic into John Nanovic's office and got into a disagreement over the appropriate byline.

Whatever the case, in mid-June of 1937, Dent submitted "Talking Toad," the first adventure of Clickell Rush, the Gadget Man.

If the subject of the Kenneth Robeson byline came up that this point, Dent was prepared to hold his ground with Nanovic. Back in 1930, he had penned a novel featuring a San Francisco reporter named Click Rush. "The Thirteen Million Dollar Robbery" appeared in S&S's *The Popular*

Magazine. A sequel, "The Phantom Lagoon," was rejected and the manuscript since been lost. Since it was his character, Click Rush's new adventures would carry Dent's name. Lester had not forgotten his surprise and disappointment when his first Doc Savage novel was published under the short-lived house name of Kenneth Roberts. No one had told him in advance.

Whether or not this Click Rush is precisely the same character is open to question. There's not enough description and background in the 1930 novel to definitely say one way or another. The chief difference was that the Click Rush who battled through "The Thirteen Million Dollar Robbery" and its unpublished sequel was a true pulp hero.

Nanovic remembered Dent telling him he'd used the character before.

> "He did do those stories for somebody else before—I think," Nanovic related. "See, he wrote a lot of stuff. I think this was a character he wrote before and picked it up and put in here. He didn't do many of them, one or two."

Whatever the case, Dent stuck to his guns——and his true byline.

"Talking Toad" lead off the first issue of the new title, November 1937. (An excerpt had run in the last issue of *Best Detective,* the magazine *Crime Busters* replaced.) Included in Volume 1 Number 1 was coupon to entice reader reaction to the new set of characters.

Response was enthusiastic. Gadget Man was consistently one of the top reader favorites, with Norgil the magician and Carrie Cashin following a close second. Ironically, Norgil came in third. With these results in, Nanovic ordered his writers to expand the lengths of their stories, and this oddball trio became the spine of *Crime Busters*.

The premise of the Gadget Man seems to be a screwball variation on the original screwball detective, Nick Charles, hero of Dashiell Hammett's popular novel, *The Thin Man*. Rex Stout's Nero Wolfe novels—which Dent also read and admired—might have also supplied some inspiration. The mysterious Bufa was Wolfe, with poor Click Rush an unwilling Archie Goodwin.

The reincarnated Rush was a reluctant hero.

Gadget detectives had been a Dent staple since his 1932 *Detective-Dragnet* series about scientific criminologist Lynn Lash. A year later, there was Lee Nace, known as the "Blond Adder," in *Ten Detective Aces*. And in 1934, Foster Fade, the Crime Spectacularist, ran briefly in Dell's *All-Detective Magazine*.

Where did Dent get this idea? Well, his mother was a great gadgeteer, capable of building crystal radios and electrical chicken-coop warmers. Dent's lifelong love of tools and gadgets stemmed from her mechanically-inclined influence.

In literary terms, inspiration can be split between Arthur B. Reeve's pioneering scientific sleuth, Craig Kennedy, and Erle Stanley Gardner whose pulp heroes often relied on simple tricks like teargas fountain pens and the like.

Headquartered in the Imperial Apartments in Manhattan's Central Park West—where Dent lived on and off during the 1930s—Click Rush roamed around the country solving crimes with gadgets and electrical devices right out of Doc Savage.

Rush had no interest in solving crimes. He was an inventor. His life goal was to sell his crook-catching gadgets to police agencies, and thereby grow prosperous. Enter Bufa.

One day Rush discovers large papier-mâché toad in his room. It comes with instructions to plug it in and insert a light bulb into its gaping mouth. Turns out it's a radio receiver that operates through city electrical wiring. The toad starts speaking:

"Hello," the toad said. *"You are, I presume, Mr. Rush?"*

Rush frowned and leaned close to the toad. "Of all the damned fool things, this mess takes the prize. Someone is crazy. Nuts."

"I am Bufa," said the toad, *"of the species* Bufonidæ, *which feeds upon snails, slugs, insects, and such undesirable things."*

"Bufonidæ," Rush growled, "is the scientific name for the toad species. What has that got to do with this insane mess?"

"I am Bufa. I feed on snails, slugs, et cetera—of the human variety."

"Sure," Rush said. "That's all right. I suppose the keepers from whatever bughouse you got out of will find you eventually."

"You don't have much imagination, do you?"

"If it takes imagination to make this seem sensible, I'm all out to-day."

There was no way, Rush thought, of locating the other person. Direction-finders would not locate a wired-wireless transmitter.

"For a long time," said the voice, *"I have been thinking of doing something like this."*

"Like what?"

"Hiring an expert private detective to investigate crimes which I think need solving."

Half of a ten-thousand dollar bill comes with the toad. Solve the mystery of the stainless steel frogs and the other half will come in the mail. Which a reluctant Rush proceeds to do.

For 18 hilarious episodes, Bufa bribes, bamboozles and otherwise bullies Rush into being his risk-taking legman. For his part, Rush vows to track down and unmask his disembodied tormentor. Their dysfunctional relationship drives the series.

When not succumbing to greed, Rush attempts to ditch the toad in various ways. Always, Bufa locates him. And the shenanigans begin anew. This combination of hard-boiled and screwball storytelling has acquired a modern appellation: "screwboiled."

The man shown examining a dummy head on the illustration heading the second story, "Death in Boxes," bears a striking and suspicious resemblance to Lester Dent himself. I doubt that is a coincidence.

The third adventure is typical. "Funny Faces" begins with the arresting first-line hook: "The man who was collecting noses had no nose himself." And so the faceless Bufa cajoles Rush into investigating a noseless man who had a mania for cutting off snoots of those who did.

The fifth exploit, "Windjam," was set in Dent's Miami dockside haunts where he used to sail. One of the best of this series, it was a salvage job. A story featuring a nautical detective named Cyrus Peace, a rustic corncob-smoking character who operated Admiralty Investigations in Miami, was rejected by *Detective Fiction Weekly*. So Dent converted it into a Click Rush story. Successfully, I might add.

This story was set around Pier No. 4, where Dent's *Black Mask* detective, Oscar Sail, anchored his sloop, and where Dent's *Albatross* spent winters.

"Les was very familiar with that spot," Norma Dent recalled. "Our boat was tied there for two winters. The boat next to ours was a cabin cruiser, owned by the Winchells, (Stewart Sterling) another well-known writer. However, he spent very little time on board his boat. Most of the time he lived in New York."

The *Four Winds* was another vessel anchored nearby. During the 1935 St. Petersburg-to-Havana boat race, Dent crewed on the 47-foot ketch, and spent six long days becalmed in the Gulf of Mexico. No doubt the *Four Winds* was the inspiration for the similarly-named *Fourth Wind* in "Windjam."

The *Albatross* spent her summers at New York's City Island, which is visited in "The Green Birds."

For some reason, toads and frogs keep popping up, as in "The Remarkable Zeke," where the recipient of a package discovers it contains a bullfrog, which he promptly stomps to death. On that thin thread, Dent hangs an entertaining tale.

All went swimmingly for two years. When Dent went to Europe, he took a vacation from Doc Savage. But he kept grinding out Click Rush tales. "The Itching Men" and "The Devils Smelled Nice" were written in Paris, and "Six White Horses," later reprinted in the 1942 *Detective Story Annual,* was inspired by Dent's 1938 European trip. One funny story, "The Monks and the Weasels," was set in LaPlata Missouri, where Dent was born, and where he lived during the final two decades of his life.

But S&S still wanted the Robeson name to appear in *Crime Busters.* So they prevailed on Dent to pen a similar series about an ex-prize fighter and reluctant detective named Ed Stone. Despite the famous byline, readers didn't take to Stone the way they had to Rush. After only seven adventures, Nanovic ordered Dent to concentrate on Click

Rush exclusively. Ed Stone wasn't "clicking," according to Nanovic.

Probably Lester Dent would have continued pounding out Gadget Man novelettes long past the period where *Crime Busters* was retitled *Mystery Magazine* in 1939, but John Nanovic made an unfortunate mistake. He slapped the Kenneth Robeson byline on "The Frightened Yachtsman."

When the story appeared in the September, 1939 Crime Busters, Dent fired off a letter to Nanovic:

> "In reading the current issue of *Crime Busters*, I noticed that the house name, Kenneth Robeson, got on one of the Click Rush yarns. I hope this is an error, because I expended considerable effort in creating the character, and I cannot consent to it appearing under any name other than my own."

Nanovic shot back that the error was actually Dent's. An Ed Stone story had been promised by Dent, but Lester submitted a Click Rush instead. In making up the cover to that issue—covers were always printed before pulp interiors—Nanovic, in his own words, "figured the best way out was to use the name Robeson on it and cross my fingers. We had no comments on it, one way or another. The next Gadget yarn, however, continues under the name of Lester Dent, just as before. That happened to be one of those things."

Nanovic guessed wrong. Very wrong. Readers may not have cared, but Lester Dent did. There was no more correspondence about the matter after that. But the one remaining Gadget Man story on hand ran in *Mystery*, December, 1939. After that there were no more.

One has to assume that Dent was so peeved at the masking of his own byline, he simply stopped writing Gadget Man. There was also a change in buying policy at that point, which would limit a writer's resale options on his own stories, and this new restriction could have played a significant role as well.

If so, this was a terrible tragedy. For this was one of the great screwboiled characters of the pulps. While Dent teased the reader with the true identity of the man behind Bufa, the ubiquitous Talking Toad, he never gave any concrete hints, not even when Rush races to Los Angeles to track down Bufa through the Continental Detective Agency—Dent's nod to his all-time favorite detective writer, Dashiell Hammett, whose nameless Continental Op worked out of their San Francisco office—and comes as close as he ever did to unmasking his tormentor. This took place in "Run, Actor, Run!' and its sequel, "A Man and a Mess."

Ironically, decades after both men had died, Hammett's daughter revealed that her father was a regular reader of *Doc Savage Magazine!* Lester would have been astounded to know that—and no doubt proud.

Alas, we'll never read the Cuban adventure promised at the end of "The Green Birds."

Nor will we ever read a satisfactory conclusion to the series. Readers have speculated that Bufa was Doc Savage or one of is aides, such as electrical wizard Long Tom Roberts. But Dent would never have mixed a series of his own with one owned by S&S, so such speculation is completely out. It's tempting to suggest that this is the philanthropic hero of his *Argosy* serial, Genius Jones. Both Jones and Bufa have a penchant for elliptical speech. Both were created around the same time.

The longest series Lester Dent ever penned, sadly the Gadget Man stories have been neglected for years. And rarely reprinted. Happily, we are changing that lamentable oversight. Additionally, we have gone back to Lester Dent's surviving carbons and restored missing text from every story that suffered editorial cuts for space and other reasons.

In 1940, artist Jack Farr adapted three of Dent's stories for Street & Smith's *Shadow Comics* and *Doc Savage Comics*. The strip was called "The Talking Toad" and Farr probably scripted them himself. Lester Dent never received credit for the feature and I suspect that it stopped after three installments because he complained about it.

As Dent's friend and fellow Street & Smith contributor Frank Gruber once said, "The Gadget Man stories were fantastic and showed a talent for invention that has not been surpassed by any other writer. Harry Stephen Keeler, perhaps, came closest but Lester Dent got as many fantastic tricks in a short story as Harry got in a complete novel."

So who was Bufa? Maybe you reading these fascinating stories can glean a clue from the adventures as they unfold....

—Will Murray

SIX WHITE HORSES

IT STARTED WITH SIX WHITE
PIGEONS—BUT IT ENDED DIFFERENTLY,
WITH SIX WHITE HORSES

CHAPTER 1
THE STIFF-BACKED MEN

IT WAS NOT six white horses when it started. It was six white pigeons.

To make it simpler, it started with one white pigeon. There was even some doubt about whether the pigeon was white. Because it was dark nighttime when the man ate it.

The man obviously did not eat the pigeon willingly. He ran into a hospital at two o'clock in the morning, screamed, "I ate a pigeon! Get it out of me!"

It developed that he had consumed the pigeon feathers and all.

He was not a large man, but he was one who would be noticed, for there was something about him—possibly the way he carried himself, with his chin pulled in and his shoulders cocked back—that gave him the manner of a man who followed a profession where it was necessary that he be stared at by people a great deal.

He also had calluses on the inside of his knees, although they didn't learn that immediately. What they—the doctors with the stomach pump—did discover was that the man had consumed a pigeon *au naturel,* feathers, claws, beak and all.

"Hide, hoof, warp and woof," as one of the doctors said.

The man died. They pumped him out; but in half an hour they were calling the coroner, who brought the police, who were responsible for reporters showing up. And so the matter got into the newspapers.

The newspaper make-up men gave it a No. 5 headline and stuck it back with the radio programs, on the theory that it was merely a case of a demented person having committed suicide, hence of no world-shaking importance.

But when another man ate a pigeon and died, it became a frontpage story, as well as a headache for the police department.

The second victim also had a backbone as straight as a ramrod and a chin that was tucked in, and he died with dignity, sitting in a police squad car which was rushing him to a hospital; and he did not scream, nor groan, and his body only gave a great shudder as life left it.

This stranger also had eaten a pigeon. But not willingly—his clothing was disheveled and his body had some bruises, indicating he had been manhandled and made to eat the pigeon by force.

The police did not identify either victim. Neither dead man's fingerprints were on file in the police department, or in the F.B.I. records in Washington; and no one could be found who knew either by sight.

It was the same with the third man who died from pigeon-eating.

This one looked like the others, not that there was much probability of them being brothers, although they all had an I'm-being-looked-at carriage and calluses on the inside of their knees. They found him sitting on a park bench, near a spot where there had been quite a fight on the grass.

The third man had only downed about half a pigeon.

At that point, Clickell Rush decided to leave town.

CLICKELL RUSH was no clairvoyant, but he got the idea the dying pigeon-eaters were going to cause him trouble.

Rush had no connection with the matter. He did not know any of the straight-backed dead men, and did not have any more idea than the police what was behind the mystery.

Rush half suspected that, in getting disturbed, he was being about as reasonable as a citizen of Kansas who dashed for his cyclone cellar when he read they were having a typhoon in the China Sea.

But Rush had had a couple of experiences with this kind of thing in the past.

So he packed up. He put a pup tent, skillet, coffeepot in a shoulder packsack. He donned an old brown hat, brown sweater, brown pants, a pair of large brown shoes that had hobnails. He bought a ticket to the end of a railroad in the Canadian woods.

Rush was going to climb a mountain, or maybe shoot a bear, or at least do something that would entertain him or make him healthy—and do it as far away as he could comfortably get.

He bought a hunting rifle suitable for bears from a sporting-goods house and ordered it delivered to his apartment.

When a crate of white pigeons was delivered instead, Rush was, in his heart, not surprised.

He was far from speechless about it. He said things that should have scorched the wallpaper the shade of brown he liked in his handkerchiefs.

The crate was small and held three white pigeons, none of which was alive. He found the crate hanging from his doorknob by a string. Who had delivered it, he did not know.

That he had better get rid of that crate, Click Rush did know.

He put it in a tin bread box from the kitchen, soldered the lid shut, doing the soldering in the laboratory and workshop in one room of his apartment where he still invented gadgets. Then he wrapped the box in stout brown paper and addressed it to an imaginary person named "Edgar Swiss," care of general delivery at the local post office, and mailed the thing, being careful not to put a return address.

Coming back from the post office, Rush saw the unconscious girl.

RUSH DID not find the girl himself. Someone else had discovered her lying in the gloom of a doorway, and a crowd had already gathered. Being possessed of a normal curiosity, Rush stopped and joined the neck-craners.

The girl was long, had hair the color of port wine, and a shape. Her face, when she was conscious, must be very alert and lively, because it was that now. She wore black, but not mourning black.

Having opened her eyes, she immediately tried to get up.

"Darn him!" she said. "Which way did he go?"

"Look here!" said a bystander excitedly. "Did some man assault you?"

The girl seemed to take herself in hand. She used her fingers to press her wine-colored hair back into place. Her fingernails, Rush noticed, were colored a wine tint to go with her hair. Only he did not think of it as a wine tint, but as ox-blood.

Since receiving the pigeons, Rush was inclined to look on the dark side of things.

"Take me to a hospital," the girl said.

As far as Rush knew, they took her to a hospital, for he went on about his business.

He spent that night in a tourist camp on the outskirts of the city, then appeared the next morning, pack on his back, to board a train for the Canadian wildwoods. He was going to ride in the day coach, because he liked the common-run, salt-of-the-earth people who ride in day coaches; and because he had learned that in paying out extra money for drawing-room accommodations, you buy little more than a state of mind. Also, he was inclined to be stingy.

The hand took his elbow as he was about to step into the day coach. The hand had some characteristics of a bear trap.

"Hey!" Rush said. "I can get on the train without help."

"The point is," said the owner of the hand, "can you get off one without being helped."

"Eh?"

"I'm a police detective."

"Huh?"

"And you can consider yourself arrested."

THE MAN had shoulders which looked as if they had been laid out with a carpenter's square from a block of oak that had been cured the way they cure boat stems, by burying in mud under water for several years. The face was broad; mouth, nose, eyes and ears were small, giving the impression that something was missing.

Almost at once, Rush noticed the odor about the man. It was a vague smell, distinct. Not body odor, or perfume, or tobacco. Something different.

Rush said, "A mistake here somewhere. The name is Clarence Ruggles. See the initials on my packsack?"

"Oh, sure," the man said. "Edgar Swiss, too, isn't it?"

"Eh?"

"You know—at the post office, there's a package addressed to Edgar Swiss."

Rush felt as if his pack were getting heavy.

"Edgar Swiss," he said.

The man said, "Edgar Swiss, Clarence Ruggles, or Clickell Rush, what's the difference?"

"But—"

The man took handcuffs out of his pocket. "We learned you had mailed a package, and we got the post office to cooperate and turn over all the packages that looked like that one. We found one with a tin box. Its bottom fitted a mark in the dust in your pantry. You should dust your pantry more often. The two pigeons inside were loaded with cyanide. Three men have died lately from eating cyanided pigeons. Now what's the moral of such a story?"

Rush said, "What's that smell on your clothes?"

The man jingled his handcuffs. "Here, hold 'em out."

Rush said, "Listen, Detective— Oh... have you got a name?"

"Lieutenant Sweet," the blocky man said. "And you're Clickell Rush, who's had some notoriety under the nickname of the Gadget Man. Pleased to meet you. Now stick the wrists out so I can put this ironwork where it belongs."

Rush thought of several things, the principal ones being jails and electric chairs. A man in jail would be in a handicapped position with regard to turning detective and clearing himself. That fact gripped his mind with cold fingers.

"You better search me," he said.

"Why?"

"To take temptation out of the way."

"Oh." The man begin taking things out of Rush's pockets. "That's a sensible suggestion."

Lieutenant Sweet took from Rush a pocketknife, money, railroad ticket; also seven small packages, no two of which were the same size. He stowed these packages in his coat, making the pockets bulge.

"On second thought," the man said, "I won't cuff you until we get outside. No sense drawing a crowd."

The day coach was at the tail end of the train. So they did not have far to walk to the station gate, where there was a long ramp that led up to doors, beyond which the waiting room was a high-vaulted white cavern that smelled faintly of ammonia, with a stone floor on which Rush's hobnailed shoes clicked and gritted.

They were half across the waiting room when Rush gave an excellent imitation of a man who had stumbled. He fell against Lieutenant Sweet, struck one of the packages in Lieutenant Sweet's left coat pocket—one of the parcels that had been taken from Rush—crushing the package.

A moment later, Lieutenant Sweet began to yell. He put back his head, then grabbed his eyes with his right hand. He struck Rush savagely, and Rush fell down.

Sweet then clutched at one of his coat pockets and began trying to empty it, endeavoring to remove one of the packages. But the package had split and mushroomed, so that it was now too big to come out. Sweet stopped tearing at the pocket and grabbed his eyes. He clutched the pocket again.

Rush, getting up and running across the waiting room, got away soon enough that the tear gas from the burst package in Sweet's pocket affected his eyes to only a minor extent.

Rush rode a taxicab from the station, and cried on his coat sleeve.

"Funny smell on that guy's clothes," he grumbled once.

Since early summer, Rush had been occupying a modernistic apartment in a new building on a street just off the theatrical district, where the sidewalks were perpetually crowded.

At the apartment-house door, there was no policeman. Nothing that looked like a plain-clothes man loitered on the sidewalk, and no green police car was parked in the block. Rush spent twenty minutes making sure.

Then he went in and talked to the apartment superintendent. The super was a small man who had a large mustache, and an appreciative recollection of ten dollars Rush had presented to him upon moving in. The ten spot had been Rush's investment against future possibilities.

"No," the superintendent said. "Positively not."

"You could be mistaken," Rush suggested.

"Not me."

"But—"

"No cops have searched your apartment," the super said. "No cops have been in this building in a week."

Rush said, "These might have been detectives, not uniformed cops. One of them maybe smelled queer."

The superintendent shook his head.

RUSH FIRED ONCE AT
THE REAR TIRES.

"Cops would've had me unlock the apartment, wouldn't they? Smell or no smell, there ain't been no cops."

Rush took out a large brown outdoor handkerchief purchased for use in the Canadian woods, and blotted his forehead.

The super looked at him.

"It's a little warm today," he said.

"Yes," Rush agreed, "it's very early in the day."

The super scratched his head with a fingernail, studied intently what dandruff he managed to scrape up, then shrugged. "I come from a long line of people who grow old and poor by minding their own business." He walked off.

Rush went up to his apartment.

The soft wax he had shoved in the keyhole before starting for the Canadian woods had been dislodged from the lock—by the insertion of a key, or a probe for picking the lock, would be a reasonable guess.

Rush struck matches, held their light close to the lock, looked for scratches inside, and found enough of them to convince him the lock had been picked with a sharp instrument.

Enough things were disturbed inside the apartment to show that it had been searched.

Missing items were: One gold watch; one high-school class ring, also gold; approximately twenty dollars in foreign money, which Rush had collected as souvenirs at various times when he was traveling.

Rush did some swearing.

"They weren't cops!" he said.

There was a knock on the front door. Rush went in haste to the back door, hoping to make a peacefully unnoticed departure down the rear stairs.

Leaning against the wall outside the back door, he found a man.

"Pardon me," the man said. "But we're looking for Arthur."

CHAPTER II
QUEST FOR ARTHUR

THE MAN WAS polite, small and old. He had a slight figure, a great deal of extremely white hair which he apparently combed straight out from his head, giving him, because of his deeply tanned face, the aspect of a Fiji Islander.

Rush moved a little to one side, studied the man's back. It was straight.

"We're looking for Arthur," the polite old man said.

"I wish I could help you," Rush said, "but—"

The man shrugged and made a slight gesture as if to button his boat. And in his right hand there was a misericord.

"Please let's not argue, he said.

Rush looked at the misericord. He happened to know it was a misericord, because he had once attended a lecture on ancient weapons and happened to remember it. The misericord had a blade long and thin, and designed to slip through a crack in a suit of armor and deliver the finishing touch to a fallen adversary.

"Back inside, if you please," the man said.

They walked into the apartment.

The knocking sounded on the front door again.

"Kindly let Hans in," suggested the man. "Doubtless he is becoming worried."

Hans was also a polite white-haired man, but taller. They were not brothers. But both combed their white hair straight out from their heads.

"Is he here, Karl?" Hans demanded quickly.

Karl fumbled with the buttons on his coat, and his misericord disappeared. The thing was carried in a coat-lining sheath, Rush decided.

"We'll look." Karl gave Rush a little bow. "If you'll pardon us."

Rush said, "Go right ahead."

They began looking for Arthur. They peered under the bed, opened the bureau drawers, then dragged the bureau out from the wall and looked behind it. Hans produced a misericord exactly like Karl's and repeatedly stuck the thick, comfortable mattress on the bed. They raised the carpet, scrutinized beneath it.

Rush asked, "Just what shape is this Arthur?"

They looked at him blankly.

"Well, is he shaped so he would be under the carpet?" Rush persisted.

"Arthur also has something we want," Karl said.

The search went on.

They found the girl in the vestibule clothes closet.

THE GIRL was leaning against the closet wall, lazy relaxation in the posture of her tall figure, something of resignation in the droop of her eyelashes.

She looked at Rush, said, "Darling, you assured me no one would look in here."

Rush swallowed his astonishment.

"Is either one of them your husband?" he asked.

The girl shook her head.

Both polite white-haired men began smiling knowingly.

"We're sorry," Hans said.

"Indeed we are," Karl agreed.

"You see," Hans explained, "we saw Arthur come into this apartment last night, and we thought he might still be here. We're very anxious to meet Arthur."

"Indeed we are," Karl agreed.

"Excuse us, please," Hans said.

"Yes, do," Karl said.

The two backed out of the front door, bowing from the waist and smirking a little. They closed the door.

Rush glued elbows to his ribs, began moving. He plunged into his workroom, going fast across the bare floor to a cabinet. Out of the cabinet he plucked a shotgun.

The shotgun was a pump type, sawed off. Rush had reloaded the shells with chemical pellets that would, if they got under the skin of man or beast, produce unconsciousness. He'd invented the pellets with the idea of selling them to police departments so they could take crooks alive, but no one had been interested.

His hobnailed shoes tore splinters out of the floor on the way to the door.

Hans and Karl were not in sight in the hall. Rush sprinted for the stairway at the end of the corridor.

Afterward, he suspected he hit the stair steps, only twice on the way down—once on the back of his neck, and once on a lower portion of his anatomy. He landed spread out beside the shotgun.

Karl and Hans came back. Karl picked up the shotgun and tucked it under his arm.

Hans said, "Such an attractive lady really shouldn't have a husband."

Karl smirked.

They walked away, moving sidewise so that they could keep an eye on Rush, Karl with the shotgun under his arm.

Rush got up, limped to the door and watched a black coupé turn the nearest corner. Through the rear window, he could see their two fuzzy white heads.

He limped to the top of the stairs to examine the wire. It was a piano wire, black, not easy to notice, and they had stretched it from a radiator to the stair banister, where it was well placed for tripping purposes.

"I hope they find Arthur," Rush muttered.

He went into his apartment.

The girl had come out of the closet and was perched on a straight-backed chair, holding a large, gray handbag on her lap. Her frock was gray that matched the bag, as were her pumps and gloves. She wore no hat, and her wine-colored hair was a wealth.

Rush said violently, "I hope they find Arthur."

She looked at him blankly. "Who is Arthur?"

Rush shook his head.

"I don't know," he said. "But I do know who you are."

"You do?"

Rush said, "You're the girl I saw lying senseless in the street near here last night."

THE GIRL with the dark-red hair looked at him steadily.

"Don't get excited," she suggested. "I'm making the rounds of the neighborhood, trying to identify the footpad who hit me over the head last night."

At first, he had thought her voice was utterly calm and natural, but now he knew it wasn't; that she was only acting, acting so well that it had taken him these two or three minutes to realize that, inside, she was as scared as a pullet watching a hawk shadow.

Rush said, "Let's tell me about the pigeon-eaters."

She opened her mouth. "What?"

"I think you can."

The girl got up and moved toward the door. "You're not the footpad who slugged me, so I think I'll be going."

Rush started for her with the same stride a swimmer uses to go out on the high-diving board.

"Hadn't you better stay back?" she asked quietly.

Rush thought so, having looked over the gun she had taken out of her dress bosom.

His mistake had been in watching her large, gray handbag. If she had a weapon, he'd supposed it would be in there. But it wasn't; and her hand hadn't gone up to fumble nervously at her throat, as he'd thought.

Rush walked past her, closed the front door, locked it, removed the key and tossed it through the living room window, which was open.

"Back door already locked," he said. "Karl locked it and took the key."

She kept the gun pointed at him. The gun was small, plain, thick, looked as if it had been constructed for the sole purpose of putting out good-sized bullets.

"Keep it aimed at me if it makes you feel better," Rush said. "And watch."

She said nothing.

"I think I know how I came to get mixed up in this," Rush explained. "I'm going to satisfy my curiosity."

IN THE bedroom closet was a stout, fat suitcase; in the suitcase was a great deal of cotton, and inside the cotton nested the statue of a toad. The toad had a green back with warts, a potty, mud-colored stomach, and eyes that had about the same expression as the eyes of a fat, bald-headed man on a front-row seat at a burlesque show. The toad's mouth was open very wide.

Rush took the shade off an electric floor lamp and after some manipulating, managed to put the bulb into the toad's mouth without unscrewing it from the lamp. He switched on the bulb. The toad looked ridiculous, sitting there with a mouthful of lighted electric bulb.

Rush looked at the girl, asked, "This business crazy enough to suit you?"

She did not answer.

The toad began making a steady humming sound, the same kind of sound made by a radio which has been switched on and warmed up ready for operation.

Rush tapped the toad with a finger and made a speech.

"I found this on my table one day," he said. "That was some months ago. It has haunted me since. There is a wired-wireless apparatus inside the toad that can send and receive over the city light wires. You can't track down a wired-wireless transmitter with a direction-finder; so there's no way of telling the whereabouts of the person who, unless I'm mistaken, will shortly talk to us through the toad."

The girl's mouth was open slightly.

"Very cuckoo, eh?" Rush asked. "The party talking over the toad will disguise his voice. Hold something in his mouth, or talk through a tube, or something. You won't recognize the voice. Matter of fact, you won't know whether it's man or woman. I don't."

The girl kept her silence.

Rush held up a dramatic finger.

"Now," he said, "we'll see if the thing performs."

Rush leaned close to the toad's ear, said, "Anybody home?"

A rather horrible strangling sound came from the toad.

"Listen," the toad said, *"do you have to bother me so early in the morning?"*

The girl was surprised enough to point her gun at the ceiling.

Rush jumped for her.

CHAPTER III

no cop

THERE SEEMS TO be grained in the nature of most men a liking for gimmicks, the average man being inclined to spend more time buying a fishing reel than he's willing to expend on an important business deal.

Clickell Rush was no exception. When he had bought his brown hobnailed mountain shoes, the spikes in the soles of the things had fascinated him so much that he had bought the shoes with the longest spikes he could find. He had confidence in those spikes.

When he started his jump for the girl, he was quite sure the spikes would dig in the floor and hold. They did not. The hardwood was too hard. The spikes slipped. Rush fell flat on his face almost exactly where he had been standing.

He rolled for the girl. She ran backward, would have gotten away except that she collided with a chair, went off balance. Rush got an ankle. It was a nice ankle. He got the girl down, they rolled on the floor, and Rush finally took the gun. He stood up.

"Poor beginning," he said in a pleased voice, "but not a bad ending."

The toad made its strangling sound, then asked, *"What in the devil is going on there?"*

Rush ignored the toad.

The girl's handbag contained lipstick, compact, comb, some cartridges for her gun, but nothing to identify her.

"Want to tell me something about the pigeon-eaters?" Rush asked.

The toad said, *"What's going on, dammit? Hello, hello!"*

The girl clamped her lips on silence.

Rush put her gun in his coat, then spread his hands.

"I'm an inventor by trade," he said. "I've invented a whole flock of gadgets for solving crimes, figuring to sell them to different police departments. But the police departments are not interested. You see, my gadgets are so fantastic the cops claim they're not practical."

He peered at the girl to see if she understood.

The girl said, "I know who you are."

The toad strangled once more.

"Hello, hello!" it said. *"Blast it, hello!"*

Rush pointed at the toad.

"That is a nut," he said. "Whoever it is, it's a nut, and it's got money. It has a mania for seeing unusual crimes solved. It has been paying me ten thousand dollars for each case. Half of a ten-thousand-dollar bill arrives before each case, and the other half shows up when the case is ended. That's all I know about the toad and its voice. Except that it calls itself Bufa."

"Hello!" the toad said. *"Hello, hello!"*

Rush continued, "It's crazy. It's as crazy as can be. But what makes it worse is this: I don't want to solve any crimes. I don't want to work for this Bufa any more. But I can't quit. The thing won't let me."

"Hello!" the toad snarled.

Rush said, "Lately, this nut Bufa has been framing me. Fixing it so I have to solve crazy crimes to clear myself."

The toad rasped, *"Who's a nut?"*

Rush went over to the toad and leaned down.

"Who sent me those poisoned pigeons?" he asked.

"*I did,*" the toad said.

"And who tipped the police I had them?"

"*I did,*" said Bufa.

Rush looked at the girl, said, "You see?"

"*Hello!*" the toad yelled. "*What's going on there?*"

Rush jammed his fists hard on his hips and glared at the toad.

"Where," he asked, "is the half of a ten-thousand-dollar bill I generally get about the time you involve me in one of these messes?"

The toad made a strangling sound that was mirthful, said, "It's time we had one on the house."

"*What?*" Rush yelled.

"*Heh, heh,*" the toad said. "*This time there won't be any ten thousand.*"

Rush walked over and picked up the chair over which the girl had stumbled just before she lost her gun. He picked up the chair, held it as high as he could over his head, carried it back to the table on which the toad sat. He took a deep breath, held his tongue between his teeth.

He brought the chair down and made the toad quite shapeless.

THE ROOM was furnished with a small, ornate, modernistic table which had cost sixteen dollars and seventy-five cents. Rush kicked a leg off this, then went around the room twice grinding rage between his teeth.

He stopped, glared at the girl and began yelling.

"Now I want the truth out of you!" he bellowed.

Being howled at suddenly made the girl mad.

"Don't squall at me!" she snapped.

"Say—"

"You clown!" she yelled.

"Listen—"

The girl kicked him on the right shin.

"I wouldn't tell you anything, you maniac!" she screeched.

He gave up, went over to the window and stood there mopping his forehead and rubbing his jaw. The window looked down into the street, and after he had been there a few moments, he noticed the man in front of the furniture-store window.

The man was bending forward from the waist, moving his head from side to side like an owl, trying to determine from his reflection in a dressing-table mirror in the window, how his face looked.

Rush said, "Well, well!" with pleased violence.

He went to the room of his apartment which he had fitted up as a workshop, and where he still invented things, and got a small suitcase which he locked, leaving the key in the workroom.

He went back and took the girl's arm.

She tried to hold back all the while that Rush was dragging her out of the apartment. Her high heels scuffed the floor, she went through convulsions the entire distance down the stairs, and in the front doorway she managed to kick his right shin again.

He was handicapped because of his efforts to keep the small suitcase out of her reach, so she could not kick it or jar it.

They walked up to the man at the furniture-store window. He had taken out a handkerchief and was dabbing at his eyes.

IT WAS the blocky man with the cured-oak face who had introduced himself as Police Lieutenant Sweet at the railway station and endeavored to arrest Rush.

Rush came close enough to catch the queer, rather unpleasant odor that pervaded the man's clothing. He said, "I want a policeman."

The man jumped, butting the show window with his head, then turned around.

"Huh?" he said.

"We surrender," Rush explained.

The girl kicked and twisted, hissed, "You fool! What—"

"*Sh-h-h!*" Rush requested. "This nice square-headed policeman will want to ask you questions about pigeon-eating men."

There was suddenly a gun in the blocky man's hand.

"I got a car over there," he said grimly.

It was a black car, a sedan, about such a machine as a police department would furnish one of its detectives. There was a foot rail across the rear floor, and the blocky man handcuffed their ankles to this.

The man then took a roll of black adhesive tape from a door pocket. He held the tape in his hands while he peered at Rush.

"Mind telling me what you think you're doing?" the man asked.

Rush said, "Mind telling me what makes you smell that way?"

The man glared, said harshly, "I asked you what you think you're doing!"

"Fooling a toad."

"Toad?"

"It's a little complicated," Rush admitted. "The toad framed me and expects to have fun watching me clear myself. I'm fooling the toad. I'm going to sit this one out."

"Sit it out?"

"In jail," Rush explained.

The man showed his adhesive tape. "Lie down," he ordered.

"Now wait a minute—"

The blocky man speared Rush with the gun muzzle, made him lie flat, then stuck strips of the tape across Rush's mouth, gagging him. He muffled the girl in the same fashion. Then he put his gun back in his clothing.

"Just to get the record clear," he growled, "I'm not a cop."

He put the suitcase on the front seat, then got behind the wheel.

CHAPTER IV
ARTHUR'S FARM

THERE WAS ENOUGH wind to shake the tops of the trees along the country road, and enough morning sunlight to make the interior of the car uncomfortably warm. The road was a dirt one, rutted, dusty.

The dust squirmed in a brownish funnel behind the machine, and there was no carpet to cover the cracks between the car floorboards; so that dust had swirled up into the machine and added another shade of brown to the outdoor clothes which Rush still wore.

Faint odor from the clothing of the burly man had pervaded the car.

Rush kept silent, made faces, and worked on the handcuff locks with the hairpin which the girl, by shaking her head violently, had managed to loosen from her dark-red hair.

As soon as he had the handcuff off, he stood up and took the blocky man by the neck. The car was grinding up a hill in low gear, so it seemed as good a time as any.

The blocky man did not excite easily. He knocked the car out of gear, yanked on the emergency brake.

Sudden stoppage of the machine toppled Rush over into the front seat with the man. The windshield was an immediate casualty of the fight. It was a shatterproof windshield, and it cracked, bulged like cardboard, but did not leave its frame. Rush slammed the man against the door, trying to stun him. The door lock ripped out, and they were in the dust.

Rush scooped up dust, tried to blind his face. The other man had the same idea. Neither succeeded.

Rush began trying to shove the other, feet first, under the car, where he would be handicapped. The result was that they were both shortly under the car, trying to bump each other's heads on the chassis, but mostly skinning themselves.

Finally, Rush got the gun. He scrambled out on one side of the car.

The blocky man scrambled out on the other side.

Rush tried to yell, "Hands up!" but only gave a loud honk through his nose. The tape gag was still in place. He tore it off.

He did not, however, yell anything.

The behavior of the blocky man took his words. The man had frozen, and was staring back along the road. He shaded his eyes with his hands, strained them.

There was another car approaching. It came fast, a coupé, and through the windshield could be seen two men who had white hair that stuck out from their heads—Karl and Hans, the pair who had been looking for "Arthur."

One white-haired man—Karl—leaned out of the charging coupé with a revolver, and a bullet passed Rush with a sound that might have been made by someone who had coughed into a flute.

Rush backed into the roadside ditch, tried to make himself as small on the bottom of the ditch as possible.

The blocky man sprang into the sedan. The machine took off.

Rush fired once at the rear tires. Then the coupé containing the two white-haired men was rocketing past in pursuit, and he fired once at the tires of that. Both bullets missed, and Karl and Hans pursued the other car over the hill.

Rush got out of the ditch eying the revolver disgustedly, selected a clod no more than ten feet away, aimed at the clod and shot. He missed the clod almost a yard.

He threw the revolver as far as he could into the adjacent woods.

IT WAS two hours later when Rush stopped a rented roadster far out in the country. He sat in the roadster a few minutes and listened to the small, portable radio direction-finder which stood on the seat beside him. He had lost time going back, but there was no help for that.

Finally, he took the "finder" headset off his ears, dropped it on the seat, and left the roadster. He walked a quarter of a mile along a dusty road, stopping often to listen, before he came to what seemed to be his destination.

The place was entered by a drive way hairy with weeds, and over the gate there was a sign that read:

ARTHUR'S FARM

The farming business did not appear to be prosperous, for paint was scabbing off the sign, the graveled drive needed work with a shovel in addition to weed cutting, and inside the gate there was a house which looked as if it was about to lie down.

All around was jungle, and a smell. The same smell that had been on the blocky man's clothing.

Rush muttered, "We better take precautions about that smell."

He took a bottle from his clothing, uncorked it, and poured the contents up and down the sleeves of his coat, and on the coat skirts. The stuff had a pungent odor that was stronger than the smell in the air.

"Phew!" Rush said.

He passed the gate up and crawled through the weeds to a point near the house, where he crouched for a while and watched the sedan in which the blocky man had been hauling Rush and the girl. The windshield damaged in the fight had been knocked out, all the glass removed from the frame.

One front door of the car was open, and Rush could see, lying on the floor, his suitcase. Doubtless the little radio transmitter inside the case was still putting out the steady buzzing signal which he had traced down with the direction-finder.

RUSH GRIMACED. He had suspected, even in the railway station, that the blocky man was no policeman. The radio had been a precaution; he had used it before to trace a quarry.

He sat and scowled about the smell in the air. It was like something that might come up if a man ate a raw hamburger and then belched.

He went into the house through an open window.

It was empty, although all the rooms had been lived in recently.

There was a huge refrigerator in the kitchen, and in it at least four hundred pounds of raw meat.

Only one other room was interesting. There were many animal pictures on the walls, also pictures of circuses and autographed photos of circus performers.

But it was the pictures of the horses and riders that made the room interesting. The horses were wonderful white animals. They were depicted doing all the tricks of the trained animals called "high-school" horses. In some of the pictures, the riders stood beside the animals.

The riders were all straight-backed men.

Labels on each picture said:

SPANISCHE RIDING SCHOOL
VIENNA, AUSTRIA

There was only one picture of six white horses together. The six white horses stood in a row, harnessed to a carriage, and the harness was incredibly elaborate. That photograph was labeled:

IMPERIAL CARRIAGE OF AUSTRIA

Judging from the autographs on the pictures, the "Arthur" who owned Arthur's Farm was a man who made his living by importing, from Europe, wild animals and trained horses for American circus use.

There was one picture of Arthur.

Arthur was the blocky man who had claimed to be a police lieutenant named Sweet.

Rush jumped violently when someone dumped something heavy on the front porch, making a loud clatter.

A voice with a pronounced Austrian accent said, "It might be that Karl and Hans would not find the harness."

Arthur said, "We won't take chances. My car is faster than that coupé of theirs, and I lost them. But they may show up.

Rush, taking a chance and looking through the window, saw that there were only two of them—Arthur and a straight-backed man—and that they were dumping harness on the porch.

CHAPTER V

HARNESS FOR SIX
WHITE HORSES

THE HARNESS WAS soiled with damp earth, so evidently it had been buried somewhere on the farm, and they were digging it up in preparation for moving it to some other hiding place.

It was the harness that was on the six white horses in the picture hanging on the wall—the royal harness for the Imperial Carriage of Austria. The massive stuff that, in the pictures, had appeared to be about all the weight the horses could carry.

Looking at the picture, it had not occurred to Rush that the harness for the Imperial Carriage of Austria might be sheathed with solid gold and encrusted with jewels.

The straight-backed man took out a handkerchief and carefully wiped dirt off the jeweled headstall of a bridle.

"It's a shame," he muttered. "All dirty."

He was a wiry man, small but athletic-looking. His face was long, and there was fear in the warp of his mouth.

Arthur staggered up with another heavy set of harness, dumped it on the porch, and stood panting.

"Dirt won't hurt it," he said.

The other shrugged gloomily. "I wish we'd never tried this," he muttered.

Arthur scowled at him. "Listen, there's a quarter of a million dollars' worth of gold in this stuff. All we have to do is melt it down, then go to Nevada, make a show of finding a gold vein, and peddle the stuff. The jewels we can have cut up later."

The other shook his head. "There's enough money in it," he said. "That's not what I meant."

"Well, stop grousing!" Arthur snapped. "We got away with it, didn't we? When Hitler marched into Austria, there was enough confusion that we got the harness out of the museum all right. And I was taking a shipment of tigers out of Austria at the time, so we got the harness out, too. Customs men don't go into tiger cages and look to see if they've got double floors. You saw that. We're in the clear."

The other put his handkerchief away. "We're not clear of Hans and Karl."

"We will be."

The straight-backed man spread his hands. "What I mean," he said, "is that we shouldn't have gotten drastic with Karl's brother."

Arthur swore violently, said, "Karl's brother was going to take half the proceeds, because copping the harness was his idea. We couldn't have that, could we?"

"We could have given him an argument."

"So what?" Arthur snorted. "We gave him a poisoned pigeon for dinner, instead."

"Yes," the other reminded ruefully. "Then Karl and Hans fed two of us poisoned pigeons. There's only you and I left. And they'll feed us pigeons if they can catch us."

"They haven't caught us, and they haven't got the harness."

"No." The other seemed cheered. "We were foresighted enough to bury the harness."

Karl came out of the weeds then.

"And kind enough to dig the harness up again," he said.

RUSH, GRIPPED by a bad premonition, whirled.

Hans was standing across the room holding, by the tip of its needle-shaped blade, the dagger which had been designed to penetrate through the cracks of ancient armor. Hans put a finger to his lips for silence.

"We found your car, of course," he said, and added, "I trust you believe me when I say I can throw this dagger as straight as you can shoot."

"Straighter, probably," Rush muttered.

"Just step outside."

Arthur and his accomplice gaped at Rush when he came out. They were standing with their hands held far up.

Hans said, "Isn't there a girl?"

"There should be," Karl admitted.

Hans went looking, and came back soon dragging the long, red-headed young woman, who kept trying to kick him, although her ankles and wrists were both handcuffed and she was gagged.

"I don't understand," Hans said, "who she is or how she got mixed up in this?"

"What about him?" Karl pointed at Rush. "Do you understand how he got in it?"

Arthur, still holding his hands up, jerked his chin at Rush.

"I'll tell you how it was about this guy," he said. "I got a note about him. It said he knew about the pigeon business, and had three poisoned pigeons. I watched him, found out he mailed a package and managed to get it. The pigeons were inside in a can from his apartment. I searched his place and found where the can had set in a cupboard."

Arthur spread his hands. "I got jittery and decided to get him out of the way. I didn't know what to think about him. The note just said he was mixed up in it. A note signed by somebody I never heard of."

Rush said, "By Bufa?"

"So you know who sent it!" Arthur growled. "How'd he find out about this?"

"Figured it out, maybe," Rush said. "Realized the men who died from eating pigeons were riders from the Spanische Riding School in Vienna, and checked up on men here in New York who might have a connection with the Spanische Riding School. You had a connection. You've bought high-school horses from the Spanische School. So maybe he sent the note to you just on a chance. Bufa's whole idea was to get me involved in this."

"Who's Bufa?"

"A toad."

All of them except the girl scowled at Rush as if they thought he was picking a bad time for a poor gag.

Rush said, "That's all right. Nobody ever believes me."

Hans pointed at the girl. "Who is she?"

"I don't know." Arthur shook his head. "I was trailing this Rush, watching for a chance to grab him and get him out of the way, on account of that note saying he knew too much. I saw the girl trailing him, too."

Rush eyed the girl, said, "So *you* were trailing *me?*"

Arthur ignored the interruption. "Last night," he explained, "I slugged her in a dark doorway and searched her. But there wasn't nothin' on her to show who she was or why she was watching this Click Rush guy."

Arthur stared steadily at Rush, but finally stopped that and turned his square, oak-hard face to the two white-haired old men. He gave them a grin that was more hopeful than hearty.

"Why not be reasonable?" he asked. "There's only four of us left, and a four-way split isn't bad. So why not be reasonable."

"We'll be reasonable," Hans said mildly.

"Very reasonable," Karl agreed in the same tone.

Arthur turned pale, the oak of his face beginning to look as if it had been out in the weather a great deal.

THE TWO old men walked them for fifty feet through the weed-and-brush jungle behind the house to an iron gate that had a huge lock and was swung from concrete posts. Other concrete posts supported a fence of woven wire that was as thick as pencils, and topped with six tense strands of barbed wire. Inside this fence were cages made out of steel and roofed over with more steel.

The white-haired men stopped at the gate and looked at Arthur.

"They're not tame, are they Arthur?" Hans asked.

Arthur opened and shut his mouth, words apparently sticking in his horrified throat.

They didn't look tame to Rush. They were tigers mostly, tigers that appeared to measure an average of fourteen feet including tails. Two cages held lions, each lion with a head that seemed as large as that of a hippopotamus.

Hans said, "Karl, I think there is some horse meat in the refrigerator in the house."

"Yes. I believe Arthur keeps it there."

"Will you get some?"

Karl departed. Hans kept a close watch on Rush, the girl, Arthur and the straight-backed man, holding his thin knife in one hand and a revolver in the other. When Karl came back, he was carrying a dish pan heaped high with raw meat.

Hans said, "I understand animals become more dangerous when they are feeding."

Arthur began to shake. "Listen, I'll give you my cut—"

"Rub the meat over them," Hans said. "Put chunks of it in their pockets."

Odor of the meat had reached the big cats in the cages, and they began to prowl. A lion roared. A tiger jumped, clung high up on the bars of its cage, then fell back to the floor, landing on its feet.

The odor of the animals, the smell that pervaded the farm and Arthur's clothing, was much stronger here.

Rush growled, "It looks like you figure on feeding us to the lions."

Hans showed his teeth viciously. "The tigers, too. They're man-eating tigers, in case you didn't know."

Karl came to Rush with chunks of the raw meat and rubbed. Rush decided that he would never again care for the sight or odor of raw meat.

"Inside!" Hans ordered harshly.

They were forced through the gate into the animal inclosure. The fence, it appeared, was a safety measure in case some of the cats should escape the cages. Two lions were roaring now, and more of the tigers were snarling.

Hans said, "We will tie them, Karl."

Karl nodded, snarled at the prisoners, "Lie down!"

Rush stared at them, asked hollowly, "You're going through with this?"

Hans nodded. "Why not? There's enough money at stake. Everyone who knows anything about it is right here."

Rush took two steps and reached the girl. He picked her up.

"In that case," he said, "I'll just walk into a cage. I don't like the idea of being tied up when they eat me."

The girl screamed, began to fight frenziedly. Rush walked backward with her, almost running to a cage.

He picked a tiger cage, the biggest one. It held six striped man-eaters, snarling and jumping against the bars. Moving fast, Rush reached the cage while Hans and Karl still stared at him, dumfounded.

"Stop!" Hans yelled suddenly, and lifted his gun.

Rush dived for the cage door, wrenched at the fastening, got it open.

The girl made gurgling voices of horror as Rush went into the cage with her.

RUSH LEFT the cage door wide open.

He kept low, dived for a concrete mound which was there for the tigers to sit upon, topped by a stump of a tree that was rutted where the big cats had sharpened their claws.

The tigers came for him, all six together.

"Scat!" he yelled beseechingly.

The cats stopped. One of them, bouncing forward in easy leaps, almost reached them, then halted so suddenly that its claws raked up sparks on the concrete cage floor. It went down flat, snarling. Then it jumped back.

Hans shrieked, "Karl! Close that cage door!"

Rush changed his course, veered around behind the tigers, got to the shelter of the concrete mound.

He took off his coat and threw it at the tigers.

"Scat!" he roared.

The tigers went out of the cage one in the lead, the others following, and Hans began to screech in terror and fire his gun as rapidly as he could pull trigger.

Rush, standing up, saw that all the tigers were out of the cage; saw also that the four men—Hans, Karl, Arthur and the other man—were interested only in their own lives.

Rush ran to the cage door and closed it.

Karl and the others had reached the fence gate, and might have gotten out safely had they not stopped to fight. Karl and Hans were trying to keep the other two men in the cage. Arthur had hold of the key—the gate lock was equipped with a key—when Hans shot him.

After the bullet struck, Arthur jumped and jerked the key out of the lock, fell to the ground, and while having dying spasms, threw the key entirely across the inclosure beyond the reach of any of them.

Rush ran back and got behind the concrete mound so he would not have to see what was happening.

IT WAS four o'clock in the afternoon before Rush's yelling drew the attention of a passing motorist, who went for the State police.

The girl was still pale. Rush had not let her get out from behind the concrete mound, and she had not wanted to after he had explained what she would see.

The tigers had not been hungry.

She shuddered. "You say they didn't attack us because—"

"Because of some stuff from a bottle I put on my clothes," Rush explained patiently. "There was cat odor on this Arthur's clothes all along, and I recognized it. Just to play safe, when I went back to my apartment to get the radio, I got a bottle of the stuff. It's a chemical odor that drives tigers and lions away. Drives away any kind of cats, in fact."

She shook her head slowly.

He said, "Seems a bit nuts, eh?"

"At least," she said shakily, "I never heard of such a thing before."

Rush grimaced. "It's one of my more sensible inventions. I sold this one, which is more than I've been able to do with the others. Sold it to one of the biggest animal trainers in the country… one of those circus guys that works in a cage with thirty lions and tigers. He says it works every time."

She frowned at him.

"If it works every time, why haven't we walked out of here, instead of sitting in this cage all day?"

Rush looked at the tigers. They were the biggest tigers he had ever seen, and they were walking around and around the cage, looking in.

"The cage suits me," he decided.

After awhile, the State police came and drove the tigers away.

Later, city police arrived, and fell to pumping the girl's hand.

"Take care of that gold harness,"the girl suggested. "Our case of the pigeon-eating men is all solved."

Rush frowned at her. "So you're a cop?"

She nodded. "Policewoman. They have them, you know."

"Yeah, but how come—"

"I was assigned to work on you. Get your confidence and find out what you knew about poisoned pigeons."

"But—"

"We got one of those notes from Bufa, saying you were worth investigating. The same kind of note that I suppose the man named Arthur got."

"You really believe there's a Bufa, and he, or it, involved me in this."

"Of course."

Rush grinned at her.

"Glory be!" he said. "First time a cop ever believed the thing. I'll give you what's left of the toad for a souvenir."

When they went to get the toad, there was an envelope lying among the remains. It was an envelope that had not been there before, plain white and without an address.

Rush's grin pushed back his ears.

"You see that?"

"The envelope, you mean?" the girl asked.

"It's the kind of envelope," Rush explained gleefully, "in which Bufa always sends the other half of a ten-thousand-dollar bill when a case is done."

Rush opened the envelope. Printing on the sheet of plain white paper inside said:

THIS ONE WAS ON THE HOUSE, REMEM-
BER?

BUFA.

THE MYSTERIOUS JUGS

CLICK RUSH, THE GADGET MAN,
FINDS PLENTY OF ACTION IN
THE MYSTERIOUS JUGS

CHAPTER I
MYSTERY AND A PLANE

CLICKELL RUSH WAS taking the brown hide off a baked potato when the telephone rang. "This," the voice said, "is the sheriff."

It sounded like a long-distance call, so Rush asked, "Any particular sheriff?"

"Why, the sheriff of the county where they had the plane disaster," the voice explained.

"What plane disaster was that?"

"A Federal Airways ship. Found it this morning. Don't you read your newspapers?"

"Not always."

"Your brother was killed."

"My brother?"

"Yes."

"Hm-m-m!" Rush said.

Rush did not have a brother.

Puzzled, he stared at the brown skin that had been on the baked potato—the plate on which the potato skin lay was a modernistic brown, the tablecloth was brown, walls of the apartment were dark brown, ceiling a lighter shade of brown, carpet a darker brown, and the curtains, upholstery, lamp shades, almost everything else, were shades of brown. Rush's clothing was also shades of brown. He liked brown.

Rush was not a large man, but he was wiry—that is, equipped with a set of muscles which looked as if they might be made out of wires. He was frequently mistaken for an acrobat or an aerialist—by men who were acrobats.

There was not much chance of his ever winning any beauty prizes, but neither was he homely enough to cause people to turn and stare at him.

"You positive this was my brother who got killed?"

"Hold the wire a minute," the sheriff said.

Rush held the receiver to an ear and waited, and wondered who was paying for the call. A chill afternoon wind shook the brown window curtains, and brought in car-horn hooting, street-car rattling and shouts of a news-boy on a street corner somewhere concerning the snow-storm in the mountains.

"You there?"

"Yes," Rush said.

In an I-am-well-and-hope-you-are-the-same voice, the sheriff said: "To whom it may concern. In case of acci-dent to the bearer, please notify my brother Clickell Rush, Imperial Apartments, Central Park West, New York City. This is the Clickell Rush who is famous as a detective. I hereby appoint him my sole heir."

"I'm a famous detective, eh?" Rush asked.

"Maybe, but I never heard of you," the sheriff said. "Anyway, what I just read you is what it says on the paper we found in his pocket."

"Paper in his pocket, eh?"

The sheriff said, "They must have missed it the first time they searched the bodies at the plane. In the morgue later on, here was this paper in one of the pockets."

"I see," Rush said.

He didn't see. He had no brother, but it appeared the words the sheriff had read over the telephone referred to himself, it being true that he had gathered some repute as a detective who employed unusual gadgets to solve crimes, at the same time it also being true that the detective busi-ness was no choice of his own—he had been trying all the time to be a plain inventor, and would have been, too, except for a toad.

The business about the toad—toad named Bufa—was so fantastic that he never told anybody about it unless he had to.

At the present time, Rush did not want to get mixed up in anything. He opened his mouth to say so.

The sheriff said, "This twenty thousand dollars cash your brother carried had us worried. Glad we found you."

RUSH CLOSED his mouth. He did not have a brother. He did not want to be a detective. But twenty thousand dollars had an interesting ring.

"Twenty thousand dollars, eh?" Rush said. "Are there any other heirs?"

"Other heirs? You should know."

"Heirs have been known to quarrel over an estate."

"Eh?"

Rush asked, "I wonder what else I inherit?"

"Say, hell, if he's your brother, you know more about that than I do," the sheriff grumbled.

The sheriff was beginning to sound suspicious, so Rush headed his questions along a different trail.

"What made the plane crash?" he asked.

"It didn't crash."

"I thought you said—"

"I said 'plane disaster.' There can be a disaster without a crash, can't there?"

Rush said, "It would be unusual."

The distant sheriff cleared his throat and talked.

"That's what this was—unusual," he said. "The plane apparently made a forced landing on this meadow on the mountains. It got down all right. There were three passengers, the pilot and the copilot in the ship. Five, all told. They must have stayed in the plane, and run the engines to keep warm, and carbon monoxide gas from the engines killed them all. Anyhow, they were just sitting there in the plane, dead as doornails, when half a dozen farmers, out tracking a wolf, found them."

Rush contemplated the telephone and thought, and it all seemed clear enough, except for the fact that he did not have a brother, nor did he know anyone from whom he would be inheriting twenty thousand dollars.

Rush asked, "Has there been a toad around there?"

"A what?"

"A toad."

"Say, are you crazy?"

"Never mind," Rush muttered. "Sorry I brought it up."

The sheriff asked, "Are you coming out here?"

"If you are sure there are no toads mixed up in it," Rush said, "I probably will."

"Well, that's what we wanted—wait, a minute." The sheriff appeared to exchange words with someone in the same office. Then he said, "They tell me they've been through the baggage that was in the plane, and found the part that belonged to your brother. We'll have that for you, too."

"Baggage? What kind of baggage?" Rush asked.

"Well, it ain't baggage, exactly. It's a lot of little jugs."

"*Jugs?*"

"About a hundred little jugs," the sheriff explained.

Rush said, "This sounds like something that should be looked into."

FOUR HOURS later, Rush stepped out of a hired ski-equipped plane and looked around at more snow than he had imagined existed anywhere in the United States this late in the spring. All about, the mountains were white humps furred with evergreen trees. Closer at hand was the hangar of the local airport, a building half-buried in the drifts, and the windsock on it hanging stiff and fat with snow.

Rush jumped out of the plane, broke through the crust, and was neck deep in snow.

"Blazes!" He looked at the pilot he had hired. "You know the stuff was this deep?"

"Hell, no!"

"What would've happened if the plane skis had broken through the snow crust?"

"Something unpleasant, probably," the pilot said. "But what are you worrying about? You're down safe, aren't you?"

Rush looked hopefully in the direction of the hangar, but there was no sign of life. A gust of wind went past, scooping up snowflakes like clouds of sugar and swirling them along.

After he had shivered, Rush reached into the plane and dragged out three average-sized suitcases. The pilot made no effort to help; the flier already was standing up in the plane, selecting his take-off route. Rush floundered with the suitcases toward the hangar. The plane bellowed, scooted up a great funnel of snow, went skiing across the field, moaned up into the lead-colored sky, and vanished by the time Rush reached the hangar.

A flurry of snow pushed Rush into the hangar office, and wind pounded coat skirts against his legs. The four men in the place—three sloppy-looking, one neat—stared at him without excitement or interest. The three slouchy men were attendants around the airport, judging from their garb.

The fourth man wore a sporty skiing jacket with hood, skiing trousers, and large black shoes that were made for hiking, not skiing. They were very flashy. They did not fit the appearance of the man who wore them, somehow.

The man in the skiing outfit was at least fifty, looked like a long wolf, and seemed the least interested in Rush of all.

Rush asked, "Where did they find the plane with the bodies in it?"

There was silence. Then one of the sloppy men moved his head slightly.

"Ten miles other side of town," he said.

"There a taxi around here?"

"Nope."

"Telephone?"

"Wire down."

"It's been *some* storm," one of the men volunteered, rather shortly.

Rush remembered the neck-deep snow outside, and concluded the explanation was rather unnecessary. The more he thought about the snow—it was cold, too—the less the idea of walking to town appealed to him, for the town, as nearly as he had been able to judge from the plane before it landed, was more than a mile distant. The town had not looked like much from the air.

About when Rush was getting to the point of thinking up choice swear words, the long wolf of a man got up and stretched.

"Well, hell," he said, "I guess I better be getting along back to town."

None of the slovenly men said anything. They were passing around a plug of chewing tobacco.

The long wolf went to the door.

"You walking in?" Rush asked.

The man looked at Rush. He shook his head. "Got a sleigh."

"Could a man hook a ride off you?" Rush asked.

The long wolf did not look pleased.

"Cost you two bucks," he said.

Rush did not look pleased, either.

"Under the circumstances—O.K.," he said.

The sleigh turned out to be a farm sled pulled by two iron-gray crowbait horses with long icicles on their whiskers. There was hay in the bed, quilts, a pile of ice-hard snowballs.

They got in, the long wolf of a man threw snowballs at the two crowbaits, and they got started. They drove half a mile, the horses getting off the road once, and the sled nearly turning over twice.

Then the long wolf of a man turned around unexpectedly. He had a gun in his right hand, a dark revolver.

"Heh, heh!" he said gleefully.

Rush looked at the gun end and his back skin began feeling queer.

"You weren't the least bit suspicious, were you?" the wolf of a man said.

CHAPTER 11

ABOUT JUGS

THE WIND CARRIED a flurry of snow over them, and the icy particles struck Rush's face with distinct impacts and made the old horses duck their tails and hump their backs.

"Get your hands out from under them quilts!" the man ordered.

Rush put his hands in plain view and let them lie in the cold.

He asked, "You know what you're doing?"

"If I don't, I'm gonna be awful surprised," the other growled.

He held his gun steady, clucked at the horses, which pretended deafness until he leaned over the sled dashboard and gave one of the old nags a wallop with his revolver, after which they galloped, snow flying. The man steered them into a lane that led to a shack, said, "Whoa!" and the horses almost fell down in their haste to stop.

"Get out," the man ordered.

The shack interior was gloomy and cold, also as bare as it could be, except for evidences on the floor that sheep and cattle had been kept in it, long ago. There was a mow up above, which appeared to contain some hay.

The two shack occupants were hump-shouldered in their coonskin coats, and blue-nosed with the cold. The coats were identical, exactly alike in every detail. The two were not twins. One man was long and swarthy, almost as long as the one in the ski suit, with thick lips. The second man was slender, not as long, very, very blond, with eyes as pale as a winter sky; he was also, except for his mouth, not much more than a boy.

"This him?" the blond boy asked.

He and his companion had been jumping up and down to defeat the cold, and they kept doing that, and beating their hands together.

"This is him, all right," growled the man in the ski suit.

"Sure?"

"Hell, I've seen his pictures in the newspapers. Of course I'm sure."

Rush looked as bewildered, and as agreeable, as he could. He put a thick Irish accent in his voice.

"Sure and begorra, you lads seem to know me," he said, "but I swear the likes of you have got me puzzled. Have we met? My name is Patrick O'Malley, no less, and I'm from Ireland no more than two weeks. Patrick O'Malley, no less, come to see his Uncle Seamus—"

"Cut it out!" said the man in the ski suit.

"Sure and now—"

"You're Clickell Rush, known as the gadget detective. Right well known you are, too."

Rush was disgusted.

He said, "Since you know so much, maybe you also know about the toad."

"Toad?"

Rush nodded. "That's right—toad."

The men exchanged glances, and one said to Rush, "You serious about this talk?"

"The toad's name is Bufa," Rush explained.

*THE BOUND GIRL ROLLED
TOO FAR AND FELL...*

The man in the ski suit struck Rush unexpectedly with his gun, struck much as he had struck the old horses to make them go. Rush fell down.

"What we're interested in," the man said, "is little jugs." **RUSH SAT** on the floor, and it felt cold through his brown topcoat, brown trousers and brown underwear shorts. In his head, besides pain from the blow, there was a singing sound such as telephone wires make in the cold. It finally went away.

"Jugs?" he muttered.

The coonskin-coated men drew guns, and all three of them gathered around him with a confidence that he did not like.

One said, "We might as well understand each other. It was a hell of a tough break for us when those farmers out wolf hunting happened to find the plane before we could get to it. So now the cops have the jugs. We want the jugs. You can get them, because of this brother stuff that was in the note they found in Crownblock's pocket."

"Who's Crownblock?" Rush asked.

"Your brother." The man laughed harshly. "Don't you know your brother?"

Rush eyed them.

"Does that brother stuff puzzle you, too?" he asked.

"It did," the other admitted. "Particularly because we don't think Crownblock had any note in his pocket when he died in that plane. But that's not the thing. The thing is the jugs. You get them for us, see."

Rush said, "Tell me one thing. How did you know I was coming?"

"Hell, don't you know we've got sense enough to tap the sheriff's telephone line, first thing? We had to know whether they suspected the truth of what happened to those people in the plane, didn't we?"

"You're telling this guy some things," one of the other men told the man in the ski suit.

"No more than he suspects."

Rush suggested, "Tell me some more."

"You go to the devil!"

The man in the ski suit kicked Rush, upset him on the floor, and while Rush was flat, suddenly stamped down hard with one of his hiking shoes. The shoe sole had long, sharp calks, and these ripped Rush's clothing and dug into his flesh.

"Ever see a man who had been stomped with calked shoes?" the fellow demanded.

Rush groaned loudly, doubled up in agony, hands pawing his chest—fingers taking off three coat buttons in quick succession, and secretly. He let the buttons fall on the floor, then heaved to his feet, grabbed the man who had kicked him, and they began to struggle. The other two men rushed in to help.

When Rush maneuvered one of them into stepping on a button, the button instantly exploded with green-blue flame and ear-splitting violence. The victim shrieked, leaped high to favor the one foot—from which most of the shoe had been blown.

It was pure luck that a second man got on another button almost at the same instant. Green-blue flash again, and a dynamite-cap crack of a sound. The man flung his arms up in shocked agony, and let go his gun. The weapon skidded into a corner.

Rush dived for the gun, got it, turned and began shooting. He aimed at the chest of the man in the ski suit, pulled trigger. He swung the gunsights to the head of one coonskin-coat wearer, yanked trigger again. The gun reports deafened him; the weapon jumped furiously in his hand. He carefully selected the part of the third man's coonskin coat that should be over his heart, and shot once more.

All three men ran out of the shack door—unharmed.

Rush scrambled over, kicked the door shut.

A young woman in the haymow, who had rolled over until she could look down through a roughly square opening, made a remark.

"As a marksman," she said, "you're simply great!"

RUSH LOOKED at the gun—it was a revolver, huge—and began to tremble in spite of himself. He broke the breech of the gun, examined the unfired cartridges, then hastily stuffed them back into the weapon.

"They're not blanks," he said.

"No," the girl said, "and the gun is a nationally used target type. I know. It happens to be mine."

Rush said, "How do you account for me missing them?"

The young woman stared at him, then said, "Might I suggest that you try it again? Maybe your luck will change."

Rush peered through cracks cautiously, and discerned the sled and three occupants. The man in the ski suit was throwing snowballs at the old horses, and they were galloping and knocking up prodigious quantities of snow.

After taking a rest through a crack, and the most careful of aims, Rush fired again. Unless he was mistaken, the bullet dug up snow not more than twenty feet from the shack, and disgustingly far to the right.

"Well, I'm consistent, anyway," he said.

The young woman had been squirming around, and now she got too close to the edge of the opening in the ceiling, and fell through. Rush leaped, caught her, although both of them ended in a rather tangled pile on the floor.

She was a rather nice armful of girl, brown-eyed, dressed in a sport outfit and red galoshes. Her gloves and her muffler were also red.

Rush untied the red muffler from her wrists. From around her ankles, he took a man's belt.

He said, "Wouldn't have to be tied up long in this weather to freeze."

"Don't I know it!" the girl said.

She got to her feet and had herself what seemed to be a really satisfactory shiver, complete with teeth-rattling.

"They have you prisoner long?" Rush asked.

"What time is it now?"

Rush consulted his watch. "Four thirty."

"Well, they got me at three o'clock. Almost as soon as I stepped off the train from New York."

"After I saw the depth of the snow my plane landed in," Rush said, "I began to wish I had taken a train, too."

"Wouldn't have made much difference."

"No?"

"They have a man watching the depot, too."

"Swell. What about the jugs?"

The girl looked in several directions in a way that was evasive. She said, "I think we'd better be chasing those three men."

"But about the jugs—"

"While we're following the men," the girl said. "There'll be plenty of time to talk."

THEY WENT outside and began plowing through the snow. It had been cold in the shack, but it was colder out in the snow, which was seldom less than waist-deep.

The sled trail was easy enough to follow. They kept in the sled tracks, for the easier walking. There was no sign of the sled—the going was a succession of brush-covered hills.

The sled was going toward town.

Rush said, "Now, about the jugs that—"

"Did they have any of your baggage in their sled?" the girl asked.

"Yes. Three bags."

The girl said something explosive and desperate, and began running, as best she could, along the snowy trail.

Rush overtook her, and they plowed along, one of them following each sled runner mark.

"What about the toad?" Rush yelled.

The girl looked at him blankly.

Rush nodded and explained, "A toad named Bufa."

She shook her head. "Now you're talking about something that *does* puzzle me."

She hurried on. Obviously, she had never heard of a toad named Bufa, and the thing was fantastic enough to bewilder her.

The toad named Bufa, Rush reflected sourly, was fantastic enough to bewilder almost anybody. It had bewildered Rush himself for—let's see, now—over a year, wasn't it?

Over a year ago, Rush had come to New York City with several trunks full of scientific inventions for catching criminals. He thought the inventions were rather good. The police considered them too fantastic to be of any value. It had gotten into the newspapers, and a reporter had dubbed Rush the "Gadget Man."

One day, he found the toad, Bufa, in his hotel room. The toad was about the size of a small bulldog, made of papier-mâché and composition, and contained a wired-radio "transceiver," an ingenius device that worked something like a radio transmitter and receiver, except that the power wires of a city's electrical distribution system were necessary to carry the communication energy. You plugged the toad into a light socket, and it immediately became possible to carry on a conversation with another "transceiver" plugged in somewhere else in the city. It was, Rush had discovered, impossible to locate that other "transceiver."

And so Bufa had come into Rush's life. The toad was fantastic, but the voice of the toad was even more wacky. The voice of the toad— Rush didn't know who it was.

Bufa was somebody with money, somebody cracked enough to want to see unusual crimes solved, and who was willing to pay ten thousand dollars for each solution. Ten thousand had looked good to Rush. He had immediately turned detective—and had spent the several succeeding months endeavoring *not* to be a detective any more.

Bufa had a distressing habit of involving Rush in a crime whenever he refused to solve one.

About this present mystery of the jugs, and the plane with all the passengers dead, Rush was suspicious. It seemed like a typical crime such as Bufa would select for him to solve. But Bufa, the toad, had not appeared in the thing, as yet.

"Look!" the girl said.

Rush looked.

"A house," the girl gasped.

The house was made of brick, had a tiled roof, was extremely neat, and smoke climbed from the chimney.

"I'll see if they have a way of getting us into town in a hurry," the girl explained.

The inhabitant of the house was a roguish young man who was all smiles when he saw the girl.

"Best I can do for you," he said, "is furnish one pair of skis."

They set out with the skis.

"You wear them," Rush said, referring to the skis.

The skis made easier going for the girl. They covered a quarter of a mile.

"About the jugs," Rush said. "It's time you told me—"

The girl drew ahead rapidly until she reached the top of a hill. Then she turned.

"The thing for you to do," she called, "is go on back to New York and forget all about jugs and everything else."

And she slid down the long hill, gathering speed—by the time Rush reached the top, out of breath from swearing, she was a racing dot, trailed by a fog of loose snow, far down the long slope. She soon disappeared.

"That," Rush said disgustedly, "is what you get for being polite."

CHAPTER III

THE EARLY BIRDS

THE TOWN WAS too small for a morgue, so the bodies had been put in the local undertaker's establishment in the back room. In spite of the cold, quite a crowd of morbid individuals had gathered and were marching through, peering at the bodies of the plane victims. The pilot and copilot still wore their uniforms.

Rush's "brother"—Crownblock—did not look like Rush in any respect. He was at least fifty years old, a very fat man, one who looked as if he had always liked good living, and had done a lot of it outdoors, judging from his healthy tan. The man's clothes were expensive.

Rush had never seen him before.

The sheriff's office was in the back of the city hall, which was four doors down the street from the funeral home.

The sheriff was a man with a face that seemed composed of jaw and eyebrows. One jowl was full of tobacco. He wore thick German socks inside six-buckle overshoes, had a huge woolly muffler around his neck, wore a muskrat cap with ear flaps, and a sheepskin coat, the outside pockets of which were stuffed with Florida travel literature.

The sheriff took a cigar which Rush offered. They grinned at each other sociably.

"I'm Clickell Rush," Rush explained. "The fellow you called on long-distance telephone."

The sheriff took three bites off the cigar, chewed for a moment, then shoved the quid over in the edge of his cheek.

"Hm-m-m!" he said. "That's interestin'."

"Here," Rush said, "is some more that is interesting. Did you know that the people in that plane were murdered?"

"The idea was beginnin' to occur to us," the sheriff admitted.

"I figured it happened this way," Rush explained. "There were six people in the plane—not five. Only five were found dead, I know. But there were six. The sixth person forced the plane down, took a rubber hose or something, and piped exhaust from the plane motors into the cabin and killed everybody. You found anything to substantiate that suspicion?"

"Rubber hose," the sheriff said.

"The one the killer used to get exhaust gas into the plane cabin?"

"Reckon so. It was hid nearby."

Rush nodded, much pleased. It always elated him to make a wildly random guess and have it turn out correct.

He said, "The sixth plane passenger—the murderer—went to get in touch with his associates. He needed their help."

"What did he need help for?"

"The jugs were heavy, weren't they?"

The sheriff nodded. "Yep. Reckon the box of jugs weighed over a hundred pounds."

"So the killer went to get help in carrying the jugs away," Rush surmised. "And the plane was found, much to his hard luck, before he got back."

"And so—"

"And so the killer is now trying to get hold of the jugs—"

"My idea exactly," the sheriff said.

He shoved his hand into one of his coat pockets, among the Florida travel folders, and brought out a cheap nickel-plated pistol that was extremely large.

"My idea exactly," he repeated.

"Huh—what?" Rush swallowed. "Say, what—"

"The *real* Clickell Rush has already been here," the sheriff said.

"Been here!"

"Got the jugs, and gone," the sheriff added.

ASTONISHMENT RAISED Rush up out of his chair, and the loud click that the sheriff's shiny gun made when it cocked caused him to sit down again.

"Say, look here!" he exploded. "Those guys—"

"You look here!" The sheriff shook his gun meaningly. "You're out of luck, because the real Clickell Rush told us you would be showing up here, trying to impersonate him and get the jugs."

Rush swallowed. "What about the twenty thousand dollars?"

"Oh, the *real* Clickell Rush got that, too."

"Made the haul complete, eh?"

The sheriff raised his voice and shouted for deputies, and two men with shotguns came in.

"We've got the murderer, boys," the sheriff said.

"Meaning me?" Rush asked.

"Yep."

"How you figure that?"

"Oh, the real Clickell Rush told as that the fellow who would show up pretending to be him would undoubtedly be the murderer."

"Did the real Clickell Rush wear a ski suit?"

"Yep."

The jail into which they threw Rush was made of concrete blocks, had a concrete slab of a roof, and it gave every promise of being very cold. The door had been standing open, and snow had drifted in. They handed Rush a shovel and watched him shovel out the drifted snow. Then they locked him in.

The bunk was a box seven feet long, three feet wide, two feet deep, full of straw. Rush sat down on the bunk disgustedly.

It was very clear that the man who had seized him at the airport had hurried on ahead and managed to convince the sheriff and get the jugs and the twenty thousand.

It was not as clear to Rush how he was going to get out of the trap they had set for him.

Nothing else was very clear about the mystery, either.

Disgusted, Rush threw himself back on the box of straw that was the bunk. Something hard dug into his shoulder. It was under the straw. He got the object out.

The thing was a toad, made of composition, about the size of a small bulldog. It had a greenish back, undersides the color of Missouri River mud, and warts.

Rush put the toad down carefully, then said three words as loudly as he could.

"*I thought so!*" he yelled.

THE LIGHT for the jail cell was an electric bulb that dangled from the ceiling by a cord. Standing on tiptoe, Rush could reach the bulb. He turned it on.

He held the toad up so that the lighted bulb rested inside the mouth of the thing, and waited. After a few moments, there was a clicking sound as the light warmed a thermostat concealed inside the toad's mouth, and this turned on the wired-radio "transceiver" that composed the toad's innards, and there was a humming while the tubes of the set warmed up.

"*Hello,*" the toad said.

Rush's voice was grim. "So you got me into this after all."

The toad said, *"I am Bufa, of the species* Bufonidæ, *feeding upon slugs and snails—of the human variety."*

That was the speech with which Bufa, the toad, almost always opened a conversation.

"That statement," Rush growled, "sounds as silly as it ever did."

The toad ignored the remark.

"When the first newspaper editions to-day printed the story of the plane being found with all aboard dead," Bufa said, *"it intrigued me. I sensed an unusual crime. So I came here in a hurry, put that note in the pocket of one of the victims—the note saying you were his brother, and should be notified. Then I sat back to watch."*

Rush was so surprised that he couldn't think of anything to say. Not that he hadn't suspected that was about what had happened. What astonished him was that Bufa, the toad, rarely explained how he got track of a fantastic crime.

"Of course," Bufa continued, *"it was unfortunate that your mysterious enemies got the jump on you. And particularly unfortunate that you are now in jail. I thought you would be there, so I went to the trouble of hiding the toad in the jail bunk for you to find."*

Rush asked, "What's in the jugs?"

"You should be more interested in what is under the other end of your bunk. Or have you found it?"

"Found what?"

"The key to the jail. You might look."

"The key?" Rush exploded.

"Goodbye," Bufa said.

Rush yelled, "Hello, hello!" then expressed himself in profanity until he ran out of breath. The other "transceiver" had been switched off.

Somewhere in the little town, the mysterious eccentric who was the voice of Bufa the toad—and Rush never had learned enough to be sure whether Bufa was man or woman—had ended the conversation.

RUSH PUT the toad in the middle of the floor, upon a little pile of straw, which made it rather conspicuous. Then he got loose snow and carefully sprinkled it in the shape of letters on the floor. He spelled out:

SHERIFF: I GOT MAD AT YOU, AND LOOK
WHAT I TURNED INTO.

Bufa the toad, made an incongruous, ridiculous and undeniably interesting object, sitting on the little dais of straw.

"Give them something to wonder about," Rush grumbled.

He unlocked the jail door with the key—it was the spare key to the jail, stolen from the sheriff's desk, if Rush was any judge of Bufa's tactics—and stepped outside. He relocked the door. Then, just on the chance that he would be confined in the place again, he tossed the key expertly through the barred opening—there was no glass—so that it fell in the straw of the bunk, out of sight.

Rush walked quickly to the railway station, and sure enough, it had a telephone booth.

"Any trains left here in the last two or three hours?" Rush asked.

"Nope. None due until midnight."

Rush went into the telephone booth, and began calling in quest of an airplane. He wanted to hire a plane, he explained, for an immediate trip.

There were no planes available. The only plane in the vicinity was the one in which the occupants had been found dead.

"How about the roads?" Rush asked.

"Blocked by snow," he was told. "Not a chance of getting anywhere until tomorrow, at the earliest."

"Is there a livery stable in town?"

"Hell, the livery stable went broke twenty years ago."

"Then where can I hire a horse?"

"Well, I don't know. The druggist has two old nags and a sled, but I think I heard a pair of fellows in coonskin coats had them rented. Only other horse I know about is the sheriff's saddle mare."

"Where does he keep the mare?"

"Why, in a shed back of the jail."

Rush breathed thanks for the encyclopedic natures of village telephone operators, and went back to the jail. The shed was easily found, and the sheriff's mare, a big black with the legs of a racer, easily led outside. Rush mounted. The horse promptly threw him. Rush got on again. And off. The third time, he convinced the horse he could stick.

He galloped out of town.

The telephone operator had told him exactly where the death plane could be found. He rode in that direction.

THE PLANE stood on a lake that was entirely frozen over, and swept comparatively bare of snow. Rush left the sheriff's horse—the animal threw him again, just as he started to get off—in a thicket of evergreen trees.

The plane was one of the big all-metal transport craft, low-winged, two-motored, as shiny as a new dollar, and as streamlined as something out of a futuristic dream.

There were State police around the craft, and snowshoes stuck in the snow nearby. All but two of the police were standing about; the two were examining the plane.

Rush began circling, using stealth, watching for tracks. It was getting late in the day, so that there was enough gloom in the woods to make tracing-finding difficult.

He saw the girl before he found her trail. She was moving stealthily, and she had a weapon, a double-barreled shotgun. From the trigger guard of the gun, a price tag dangled, so evidently she had purchased the weapon in town.

The girl crept along for fifty yards or so. Furtively. Rush prepared to quicken his pace and catch up with her.

One of the men in coonskin coats came lunging from behind a tree and fell upon the girl. Her shotgun did not explode. He got a glove over her mouth before she could cry out.

They struggled on more or less even terms, until the other coonskin-coat wearer, and the long wolf of a man in the ski suit, and a fourth man wearing a gray-and-blue mackinaw, came charging out of the underbrush and helped with the girl.

By the time the fight between the girl and the four men had ended with the girl overpowered, Rush had crawled close enough to catch their voices.

"This makes it swell," one of the men said savagely. "Besides this girl, nobody else knows what it is all about. We get rid of her, and we're clear."

"What about this other bird—Click Rush?"

"What does he know?"

"About the jugs."

"He doesn't know what is in them. And he probably wouldn't know what the stuff was, even if he'd seen it, which he didn't."

The other made a grumbling noise which did not convey anything except that he was not entirely satisfied with the situation.

The man in the ski suit snorted. "Hell, it's perfect," he declared. "Crownblock takes off by plane with the samples, and I'm aboard. He doesn't know me by sight. I look up the route of the plane, and telephone you fellows to be at this little town. When we get over the town, I spring a gun and force the pilot to bring the ship down."

"I suppose everything went perfect from there on," muttered the other.

"Maybe it didn't. But it came out, didn't it? Maybe Crownblock did spout off until everybody in the plane knew who I was and what was up. But I fixed that. I was all prepared, in case I had to do that. I had the rubber hose in my handbag, ready for the job. Only I couldn't carry the jugs afterward, through that snow, and while I was gone after you fellows, them blasted farmers found the ship. Anyway, we've got the jugs now, haven't we?"

One of the men had moved a few yards and scrambled up a tree. He peered intently.

Now this scout returned.

"All the cops are going but two," he explained. "They're putting their snowshoes on."

That was obviously what the men had been waiting for. They became grimly silent; ten minutes passed.

"Waited long enough," a man muttered. "It'll be getting dark. I've got to have light to lift that plane off. And we've *got* to have the plane. It's the only way of getting out of this hole."

"What about the girl?"

"Hell, she's Aimee Gordon, and she works for the same company as Crownblock. Has charge of the New York office. She dashed out here when she heard the plane was down. And she surmised we'd be trying to grab this plane to make a break—"

"What I meant," the man said, "is what do we do with her?"

The man in the ski suit took a deep breath.

"I'll stick with her," he said. "The rest of you walk toward those cops. They won't suspect anything. When you get close, blast the cops. I'll shoot the girl. We'll take off."

It was so simple that none of them had any questions or objections.

They had gagged the girl. Now they made sure that the gag was forced in her mouth very tightly, then examined their mufflers which they had tied around her wrists and ankles.

"You better sit on her," one suggested.

The man in the ski suit sat on her.

The others walked away in the direction of the plane.

Rush took the wrist watch off his wrist—it was a watch that looked large, even if it was streamlined—and opened the thing. The mechanism of the watch was very small, actually occupied but a fractional part of the case. He put the works in his pocket. Then he flipped a lever in the watchcase—it instantly began to buzz—and threw it.

The watchcase landed in the snow where Rush intended—about a yard from the man in the ski suit. The man heard it strike. He stared at the spot curiously. He was about to lean over when the case exploded.

The blast was terrific, knocked the man completely over. Snow jumped up in a great cloud.

Rush made his voice as loud as he could, in the direction of the plane.

"Watch out for those men, cops!" he yelled at the top of his voice. "They're killers! They're going to shoot you!"

IT WAS hard to run in the snow, but Rush did the best he could. Snow hurled up by the trick grenade was still a cloud, and he plunged into the falling particles, fell upon the man in the ski suit. The fellow had lost his gun. Rush had seen it fly away after the blast.

Rush closed with him. The man was taller, also strong, a man who had done a lot of physical work. He wrapped his long arms around Rush, proceeded to demonstrate that he knew something about wrestling. Rush tried to punch his jaw, failed. The man was holding him too close. The fellow brought up a knee. Rush howled. They swapped ends in the snow.

Rush changed his tactics, pushed the end of his necktie in the man's mouth. The man seemed to approve. He bit down on the necktie, proceeded to hold Rush in that fashion, and slam him with fist blows.

From the lake ice, shots came. Two of them. Then four or five—it was impossible to tell how many, because echoes bounced back from the hills and made a great gobbling.

Rush and his foe got to their feet, fell down. They tumbled across the girl, and she began kicking them indiscriminately.

Suddenly, Rush's victim howled. He spat out the necktie end.

But he had been a little too late in discovering that the necktie end was loaded with a chemical that would produce abrupt unconsciousness—another of Rush's gadgets.

The man did not go to sleep immediately. He knew he was weakening, so he devoted all his efforts to getting away. Rush let him go, and while the man ran, waded over and kicked around in the snow hopefully for the man's gun.

Before Rush found the gun, one of the men in coonskin coats came charging out of the brush. There was no sign of the other coonskin wearer, or the fourth man in the mackinaw. Bullets chased the runner, whacking the frozen bushes, screaming and knocking down snow.

The runner in the coonskin coat was looking backward fearfully.

Rush had presence of mind to pitch forward in the snow, burying himself. When the runner's footsteps were close to him, he jumped up. The fellow saw him, swung his gun. Lunging, Rush got hold of the weapon with both hands, twisted, and milked it out of the other's clutch.

Rush clubbed the man several times with the gun before he discovered that it was the deep snow that was keeping the fellow on his feet.

The man in the ski suit had stopped and was turning around and around foolishly, and now he fell.

IT WAS ten o'clock that night, beside a pleasant roaring fire in the town hall, before Rush got his explanations repeated sufficiently that they were believed.

"You see, they grabbed my baggage, and that handicapped me," he explained. "Practically all my gadgets were in the baggage."

"We see everything perfectly," the sheriff said, "except that business about the toad. We don't believe that."

"Skip it, then."

"But it's important—"

"Not half as important to you as to me!" Rush said grimly. "Some day, I'm gonna find out who the voice of that toad is. And boy! What a day that'll be!"

The girl came in. She had both hands full of small glass jugs, and the jugs appeared to contain rock dust. She put the jugs in a suitcase, went out, and came back with more jugs.

"Do I ever learn what those things are?" Rush asked.

She smiled at him. "Didn't the sheriff tell you?"

"He hasn't done anything but listen."

The girl held up one of the jugs. "What does the contents look like?"

Rush said, "Rock dust."

"That's right."

"Huh?"

"The jugs contain core samples," the girl explained.

Rush shook his head, said, "A core sample may make sense to you, but it's just gibberish to me."

"These samples were taken from a well that is being drilled for oil," the young woman elaborated. "Any good geologist can examine them, and tell exactly what strata of rock the well has been drilled through at any given depth—and from that, judge very accurately whether there is a chance of hitting oil."

"That makes them valuable, eh?"

"Of course. Rival oil operators, if they have these samples, can tell whether land around our wildcat test well is worth leasing. These core samples can make several hundred thousand dollars for lease speculators. We have a sure-fire well. These samples prove it. Those men who were after them were lease speculators."

"Where is this test well?"

"In Kansas."

Rush asked, "Then what were the samples doing in a plane headed for New York?"

"Our geologist," the girl explained, "is in New York. The samples were being rushed to him. He needed them to prove how good the test is, so our company could borrow some money."

She finished carrying in the jugs, and made a last trip, on which she brought a sheaf of greenbacks—the twenty thousand dollars—which she tucked in the suitcase with the jugs of core samples.

"That goes, too?" Rush asked ruefully.

"Of course. The money belonged to Crownblock—his life's savings. He was going to invest them in the company when he got to New York, he had explained."

Rush was of the private opinion that the idea of so much trouble over core samples was slightly screwy, but kept the idea to himself, for the reason that he considered his own inventions as perfectly sensible, whereas everyone else thought they were wacky, which might mean that his judgment was askew.

A deputy sheriff came in, holding an envelope and looking puzzled.

"We found this under the door," he said.

It was addressed to Rush. The envelope contained a ten-thousand-dollar bill—the sum that came to him from Bufa, the voice of the toad, each time he solved an unusual crime.

Rush yelled, "Blast it!" and rushed out and began hunting around in the snow for tracks that Bufa might have left.

As he expected, he did not find any footprints that he could follow.

"Some day," Rush muttered, "one of these messes is going to end differently."

THE MINKS AND THE WEASELS

IT SOUNDED LIKE A SKIN GAME TO CLICK RUSH!

CHAPTER I

UNCLE JETHRO

CLICKELL RUSH DID not know he had an Uncle Jethro. Before the thing got finished with, he was not at all glad that he had found out that he owned an Uncle Jethro. In fact, he would much rather have not. It came about as follows:

The sign over the door said *Palais de Plaisir*. But regardless of that, it was the best restaurant in town.

Clickell Rush got out of a taxi, went inside, looked as important as he could, and gave the head waiter five dollars. Rush was shown to the best table in the place. He ordered champagne, seven dollars. He ordered rock crabs, three dollars and a half. Rush was on a splurge. He was blowing himself. He did not, however, have a girl along, for that would have doubled the bill, and he saw no sense in doubling a bill of champagne, seven dollars, and rock crabs, three-fifty.

Clickell Rush was celebrating the fact that a toad had not molested him recently.

Not a toad in his life, for weeks. He did not tell anybody why he was celebrating, having a pretty good idea of what they would think. Toad? Nuts, they would say. Bats in the belfry.

"This is the life," Rush said, expansively.

He wore his latest big idea. It was a full outfit of evening clothes, tail coat and all. It was brown. Everything brown. The conventional color for such a monkey suit is deep black. But Rush liked browns. People stared at him.

The champagne came.

The floor show started with a loud fanfare of music from the big orchestra and a burst of brilliantly colored spotlights and a string of high-kicking chorus girls who wore no more than the law allowed and another girl behind a big bubble who wore considerably less than that, who proceeded to dance around the stage in a very, very deep silence, as if all the gentlemen present might have their breaths bated lest the bubble burst.

Uncle Jethro arrived about this time. Uncle Jethro gave the head waiter a fifty-dollar bill. He gave the waiter a hundred-dollar bill and said, "I want *service,* my boy." He peeled the fifty-dollar bill, and the hundred-dollar bill off a roll of their brothers that would choke a hippopotamus.

Rush began to feel like a piker with *his* splurge.

The old gentleman wore a checkered vest with a diamond watch chain, a lavender shirt with diamond studs, a purple necktie with a diamond pin. He had a big pleasant face. But he was no beauty, because he had billygoat whiskers. He was about as tall as Rush, or around average height.

"Yippee!" Uncle Jethro said, ogling the chorus girls. "It wasn't like this in Missouri!"

Uncle Jethro took out his roll. He began wrapping fifty-dollar bills around cubes of sugar, and throwing them at the chorus girls. Every time he hit a cutie with a fifty-dollar bill, he would yell, "Yippee!"

This sort of thing rather played hell with the show.

No telling where it would have ended up, if Uncle Jethro hadn't looked around and spied Rush.

"My nephew Clickell!" Uncle Jethro hollered. He rushed over. He threw his arms around Rush. "I'm your Uncle Jethro from Missouri!" he shouted.

Rush had never seen the old goat before.

RUSH WAS a mite put out with Uncle Jethro by now for several reasons, one of them being that it was hard on the ego to have one's own private splurge made to seem mere miserly piddling, and another reason was that if Uncle Jethro was in the family, it was a shame for all those fifty-dollar bills to be thrown at chorus cuties.

"My nephew Clickell!" howled Uncle Jethro.

"Nonsense," Rush said.

"I am your Uncle Jethro!" yelled Uncle Jethro.

"I have none such," Rush said.

Everybody was looking at them. The chorus girls were crawling around on the stage like gophers, seeking lumps of sugar with fifty-dollar bills for skins, and there began to be hair pulling.

"Don't you remember your aunt Mame?" bellowed Uncle Jethro.

Rush did. Suddenly, he remembered. Mame was his aunt who had run off with the traveling man a long time ago. Rush had not heard of Aunt Mame in years.

"Oh, gosh!" Rush said. "Uncle Jethro!"

Uncle Jethro kissed Rush on both cheeks.

"Nephew," yelled Uncle Jethro, "I am proud of you! I love you! You are the apple of my eye. I've read in them there newspapers about you."

"How is Aunt Mame?" asked Rush, embarrassed.

Uncle Jethro wiped a quick tear from his eye. "Aunt Mame passed on to her reward years ago, nephew," he said.

Uncle Jethro kissed Rush again, on the forehead, so that the goaty whiskers got in Rush's mouth.

"Nephew, I love you," he roared. "I am proud of you. I am very rich. I am so rich I stink of money. I want you to be my heir."

"What did you say?" Rush asked.

"My heir. I want you to be it."

Uncle Jethro dug around in his hip pockets.

"Here, nephew." He presented the package. "My will. It makes you heir to all my riches. Do not open it until I die, however."

With a glad shout, and another, "Yippee!" Uncle Jethro bounded away. "Goodbye, Nephew Clickell," he screeched. And he was gone in the crowd. He vanished. The chorus girls all looked very disappointed.

Rush sort of collapsed in a chair.

RUSH TOOK home the package Uncle Jethro had given him and put it on the table and sat looking at it. So it contained a will, eh? Did wills mention how much was willed? Rush felt a great curiosity, but it was tempered with restraint, because Uncle Jethro had insisted that the package not be opened while he was alive.

Unfortunately, poor Uncle Jethro did not live long.

The newspapers told about it the very next morning. They told how a motorcycle cop had seen the burning car, and reached the accident too late to do anything, and there was even a few words from the cop to describe how hot the fire had been. "It was a blazing inferno," the cop said. The car had hit a gasoline truck that had been standing parked beside the highway while the truck driver took a tire to be fixed.

All that had been found in the car was a charred bone or two, a diamond watch chain and a set of diamond studs and a diamond necktie pin, with mountings more or less the worse for melting. And a gold watch, turnip type, engraved, "Jethro Milligan, La Plata, Missouri."

Uncle Jethro had burned up in an automobile accident.

Clickell Rush slumped in a chair. Last night's performance by Uncle Jethro had been very funny, but now suddenly it was not at all funny. It was sad. Rush felt extremely low. When you are able to throw away money the way Uncle Jethro was throwing it, and have a time the way Uncle Jethro was having one, it must be hell to have to die.

Clickell Rush opened the package that Uncle Jethro had given him. The will was inside. The will was sort of queer. It was a little picture frame about three inches wide and six inches long, and under the picture glass was a piece of white paper with some typewriting on it. The typewriting read:

> *My Nephew Clickell Rush:*
>   *Go to the bridge over Titus Creek two miles northeast of La Plata, Missouri, and walk one hundred and thirteen yards west.*
>
> *Uncle Jethro.*
>
> *P.S. Bury me there, too.*
>
> *U.J.*

Rush wiped a tear from his eye, then looked in his closet where there was nothing but brown suits, and put on the darkest brown one for mourning.

Rush went and argued with the coroner for a while and the coroner gave him Uncle Jethro's bones in a tin box. Rush got ready to take the bones to Missouri. He packed.

After some thought, and rather reluctantly, Rush packed the toad.

He had no idea, of course, what he was getting into.

THE TOAD was about of a size to go in an average suitcase conveniently. The toad was green on the back, had a mud yellow tummy and warts, and a mouth that was always open, and little glass eyes that always looked as if they had just seen something funny and wicked. The toad was made of papier-mâché or some such composition; Rush didn't know what kind of stuff it was made of, exactly, because he hadn't constructed the toad. He didn't care, either.

He manfully resisted an impulse to take a hammer and beat the toad into a pulp.

Rush decided to take an airplane to Missouri. He wanted the airline people to stop the plane at an emergency government airways field located at a place called Millard, which was close to where he wanted to go, but the airline people demurred.

"I am Clickell Rush, known as the Gadget Man," Rush said modestly.

The airline people said, "You mean you are the fellow who has invented a hundred thousand unusual gadgets for catching crooks?"

"It was only about five thousand gadgets," said Rush.

"You are the fellow who tried to sell his gadgets to the police departments without any luck, so you went into the crook-catching business using your own merchandise, and you have recently acquired quite some reputation for solving amazing and unusual crimes?"

"I did not willingly become a detective," Rush said. "In fact, I am trying very hard not to be one. But a toad keeps thwarting my desires. Yes, a toad. No, never mind the toad. I am embarrassed by the matter. Yes, I know it sounds crazy. How about stopping your plane at Millard to let me off?"

"Can do," the airline people said, impressed.

As a plane flew him toward Missouri, Rush cogitated. Most of his thinking was about the toad. How silly it was. Months ago, he had found that toad in his room, with some bait—very effective bait—in the form of one-half of a ten-thousand-dollar bank note.

Rush had learned the entrails of the toad consisted of a very efficient wired-wireless device which was best called a "transceiver," for the contraption, when a lighted electric bulb was placed in the toad's mouth, enabled someone somewhere in the city to talk through a loud-speaker in the toad, and Rush could talk back by speaking into a microphone also concealed in the toad.

There was no way of telling where the voice of the toad came from. Doubtless the individual was speaking over a similar "transceiver."

The voice called itself Bufa. It frequently said, *"I am Bufa, of the species* Bufonidæ, *which feeds on slugs and snails—of the human variety."*

Rush had been tempted by the half of a ten-thousand-dollar bill into solving a fantastic crime with his gadgets, and he had received the other half of the bank note, and also had come near getting his head shot out from between his ears. Other unusual crimes followed, on the same terms. Rush got shot at, stabbed at, bombed at, poisoned at, which made him scared and disgusted, so he tried to quit.

Rush hadn't been able to stop solving unusual crimes for Bufa, so far. Bufa had a diabolically clever way of framing him into spots where he *had* to solve unusual crimes, whether he wanted to or not.

Rush did not know who Bufa was. He had not been able to find out. He would've liked to. He planned to walk on Bufa's face.

The plane got to Millard. A farmer had a Model T, so Rush got to the bridge over Titus Creek two miles northeast of La Plata and walked one hundred and thirteen yards west into some woods, as Uncle Jethro's strange picture-frame will directed.

He found a man behind a bush, a man with a shotgun and two large hound dogs. Unluckily, Rush did not discover the man until the fellow came bounding out from behind the bush.

"Sick 'im, Bowser and Howser!" the man yelled.

The two pothounds proceeded to take Rush's legs in their mouths.

CHAPTER II

BOWSER AND HOWSER

BOWSER AND HOWSER were two large brindled hound dogs with man-eating desires and the noise-making capacity of two hungry lions. Rush swore and fell down. Birds began flying out of the woods, frightened by the bedlam.

"Take 'em off!" yelled Rush.

"Hold 'im, Bowser! Hold 'im, Howser!" The man with the shotgun proceeded to search Rush.

The man was long and bluish, like his shotgun. That is, his beard was stubbled and bluish, while his nose was large and red, like an apple, and his mouth was wide and full of teeth that were tobacco stained, like walnut pegs. He wore gum boots, overall pants, mackinaw coat, a cap with ear flaps. He found Uncle Jethro's will.

"What is this?" he asked.

"That," Rush said, "is Uncle Jethro's will."

The man sniffed and stuck the picture-frame back in Rush's coat pocket. "We don't go for humorists around here," he growled. "So don't start smart-Aleckin' with me."

"Are you related to Uncle Jethro?" Rush asked. "Are you a disappointed heir, maybe?"

"Disappointed. Don't know about the heirin' part."

"Don't you even *know* Uncle Jethro?" asked Rush.

"Sure," said the man with the shotgun and hound dogs. "Don't know nothing about heirin', though. But if that's your story, stick to it. 'Specially if it entertains you. My name is Slim."

"Your name is Slim what?"

"Just Slim will do." The man picked up a club. "Get away, Bowser! Get away, Howser!" he yelled. The pothounds released Rush's legs, backed away, licked their chops and seemed disappointed.

Rush got up. "Thanks," he said.

"Don't mention it. I just wanted to be sure Uncle Jethro sent you. Come on."

Rush looked around. There didn't seem to be anything in sight but buckbrush and scrubby, shagbark, hickory trees, and if this was Uncle Jethro's heritage, he decided he didn't want any of it.

"Come on," said Slim.

"No, thanks," said Rush. "I'll just be getting along to town for some iodine and other dogbite medicine."

"Come on." Slim held his shotgun so Rush could look down the barrels. "It's all right. I'm the feller you come to see. Anyhow, this shotgun goes off easy."

Rush followed Slim. The pothounds, Bowser and Howser, snuffled along behind, showing their teeth. They all jumped a gully; beyond this was a thicket of denser brush composed in no small part of scrawny thorn trees and wild blackberry and gooseberry bushes.

In the brush was a shack, probably a farmhouse that had not been used in a long, long time. Where the weatherboarding was off, the plaster and lath showed through, and the whole structure leaned to the south, in a tired way, as if, with a trifle of encouragement, it would fall down. There were two shabby rooms.

In one of the rooms was a short and wide man wearing coveralls and a man who was not so short and dressed rather like a sport in a collegiate bush jacket which looked as if it had cost, at the most, ninety-eight cents.

The door into the other room was closed.

"Here's our city slicker," said Slim, meaning Rush.

"Hy'ah, slicker," said the bush jacket.

"Let's get it done," said the short one in coveralls. "Will you use a gun?" he asked Rush.

"He hasn't got a gun," said Slim.

"What does he use—his hands?"

"Use my hands for what?" asked Rush.

"To kill the girl," said the bush jacket.

Rush swallowed three times so fast that the swallows sort of piled up in his throat.

"Was the job of killing a girl what I inherited from my Uncle Jethro?" he asked.

"WAIT FOR ME," A VOICE SAID.

"You might put it that way," said Slim.

RUSH DID not like the looks of his new acquaintances. On the other hand, he could tell from the way that they looked at him—as if he was a polecat they had met on Sunday—that they didn't think much of him.

THE VOICE CAME FROM A GIRL ON THE RAFTERS.

Rush was confused and puzzled by the situation. Likewise, Slim and the other two men did not act as if their minds were exactly at ease.

"You sure this is the feller, Slim?" asked the bush jacket.

"Sure."

"Why?"

"On account of what he had in his pocket," Slim said. Slim turned to Rush. "Show them… er… Uncle Jethro's will, slicker."

Rush handed over the picture frame. The bush jacket turned it and eyed it, then gave it back. "One hundred and thirteen yards west of the bridge is the spot we were to meet you," he said. "But what about this postscript: 'Bury me there, too'?"

"Maybe Uncle Jethro meant for him to bury the girl there," said Slim. He turned to Rush again. "What about that, slicker?"

Rush said, "If it's agreeable all around, let's just call this off and I'll go back where I come from."

"Huh?" said Slim.

"The hell with Uncle Jethro's inheritance," said Rush, "if you get what I mean."

"You can't do that." Slim shook his head. "You can't say the hell with it."

"No," said the bush jacket. "You got yourself a job. We think you're the dirtiest, stinkingest, lousiest, slimiest thing that ever crawled out from under a log. You probably think we're apple knockers with no guts. That ain't got nothing to do with it. You're going through with it. None of us had the stomach to kill that girl. Not even Uncle Jethro, old rip that he is. You were sent here to do the job. Like I said, and like Slim here said, you're going through with it."

"I'm beginning not to like Uncle Jethro," said Rush.

"Who likes the old rip? So what?"

"So I think there's been a mistake," Rush said. "I am Clickell Rush, known as the Gadget Man."

"Gadget Man?"

"Know what a gadget is?" asked Rush.

"Hell, no."

"Look," said Rush.

Rush took a brown silk handkerchief out of the upper pocket of his coat; it was very large, apparently made of a peculiarly shiny silk that crackled, and consisted of two thicknesses. He tore off one end, which converted the handkerchief into a sort of sack. Rush drew the sack over his head and tied it around his throat, in a way he had practiced.

"What is this?" growled Slim.

"Witchcraft," Rush explained. "I'm a he-witch."

Rush pulled a button off his left coat sleeve, another off his right coat sleeve, and put them together on the floor. He stepped on the buttons. They crushed together and mixed. They sizzled. They gave off bluish fumes.

"The witch's brew," announced Rush. "If you will look closely, you will see a little green devil ringing a bell."

The three men gathered around the smoke. They started to look.

"Damn!" yelled bush jacket.

"Tear gas!" squalled Slim.

Rush began to move around fast.

THE HANDKERCHIEF-SACK over Click Rush's head—the handkerchief was impregnated with a compound that gave it the airtight and transparent qualities of Cellophane—formed simply a temporary gas mask, for it was possible to breathe inside the thing for a short time until the oxygen ran out, and there was not great difficulty in seeing through the treated fabric.

Rush was a wiry, and extremely muscular fellow for his height, and was often mistaken for a circus or vaudeville acrobat by persons who were themselves acrobats. Nor was this the first fight in his life.

Diving in, Rush slugged Slim behind the right ear, and Slim fell down; all the time Slim was holding his hands to his eyes, even after he hit the floor; at the same time he was holding his shotgun clamped in his arms.

Rush grabbed the shotgun. He started to hold it so it was ready to shoot; the next instant, it went off. Slim was right about it being easy on the trigger. The shot hit the ceiling. Practically half the plaster on the old ceiling fell on their heads.

Bush jacket and the other man were jumping around and grinding out profanity. One held a revolver. He could not see well enough to use it.

Rush realized both barrels of the shotgun had gone off. He broke into an instant cold sweat, remembering the careless way Slim had pointed the blunderbuss at him.

The man holding the revolver began to shoot at random. Rush skipped about, trying to keep behind him. He slugged the fellow, but not successfully, and the man wheeled and nearly put a bullet in him.

Rush made his voice as loud as he could.

"Hurry, sheriff!" he roared. "They're all in here! Come on, sheriff! Quick!"

The men became very still. In spite of the tear-gas agony, they looked scared.

"Quick, sheriff!" Rush shouted. "They've got a dose of tear gas. They're helpless!"

Slim said, "Oh, hell! He's law!"

"Me, I'm running," rasped bush jacket.

They were blinded and a little turned around and they had trouble finding the door, but Slim finally located it, called the others, and they joined hands. Away through the brush they went, holding hands.

Rush grabbed the shotgun and started to follow. He charged out into the sunlight. Then he stopped.

"What the blazes am I doing?" he asked himself.

He tried not to feel excited and bloodthirsty. He tried to convince himself the thing to do was not pursue this any farther. "The thing is to get out," he said. "The thing to do is go far away from such a screwy mess."

He went back into the shack, the shotgun tucked under his arm, and kicked the fizzing tear gas chemical outdoors. Then he looked the place over. This room had been lived in, but not very comfortably—there were three folding cots and a pair of apple barrels for furniture and numerous empty canned heat tins that had been used for cooking.

The door into the other room was padlocked. Rush kicked it and spoke loudly.

"Hello, in there," he said. "The war is over."

No answer.

Rush used another of his gadgets on the padlock: He thrust two fingers up in the end of his necktie, inside the lining that is in most neckties, and pulled out a string. A thick string. He worked the string into the padlock; he poked the last bit in with a match. He tore a hole in the lining of his coat and fished out what looked like a match head. He poked this in the lock, too. Then he stood back quickly.

The explosion was deafening. Louder than a shotgun. The string was chemical-saturated, and the lump of another chemical that looked like a match head had made it explode. It was somewhat the same effect as guncotton and a detonator. The pieces of the lock flew about.

The door into the other room flew open.

"You can come out, girl," Rush said.

No one came out.

Rush went in and found a box. He opened the box and there was a dead man.

CHAPTER III

INNOCENCE AND
THE SHERIFF

THE MAN IN the box was a long fellow, probably with a very pleasant face and a rather ruddy complexion, although it was difficult to say about the last, because from all appearances he had been in the box some time. He wore corduroy trousers, laced boots, a hunting jacket, and a corduroy hunting cap was in place on his head. The hunting jacket had large game pockets and the head of a squirrel was peeking out of one of these. The squirrel had been shot between the eyes. So had the man.

"Ugh!" Rush said. "Whew!"

He became pale. His hands felt as if they held melting ice. His legs began to feel as if the bone had been taken out. Rush did not care for corpses in the least. The fact that he had seen several in the past did not help; in fact, the distressing effect seemed to get worse each time.

"Oh, my!" Rush said.

He turned around with the idea of running out of the shack. He stopped when a voice addressed him. It was a frightened voice.

"Wait for me," the voice said.

She was on the rafters. She had jumped, probably, and chinned herself, then climbed on top of the rafters, where she was crouching. There was no plaster or laths on the ceiling in this room.

She was trembling so that it was evident there was danger of her falling off the rafters.

"Here, let me help," said Rush.

He got her on the floor. Instantly, she wrenched herself from him and dashed out of the shack. Rush ran after her, taking off the handkerchief gas mask. She stopped outside.

"I couldn't bear to stay in there another instant!" she choked.

"How long," asked Rush, "have you been in there?"

"Four days," said the girl wildly. "Four days, while they tried to get someone unscrupulous enough to kill a girl."

Rush glanced about uneasily, but there was no sign of the three men who had rushed off after they had been blinded by the tear gas. But they might come back.

"Let's git," the girl said.

"Yes, let's," agreed Rush.

They ran through the woods. Rush remembered that the farmer with the model T whom he had hired at the Millard airport was waiting on the road, so he guided their fast steps in that direction.

"This is a dickens of a mixed-up thing that doesn't make sense," Rush said. "I don't see why such things have to keep happening to me. After all, I never did anything but invent some gadgets."

The blackberry and gooseberry bushes scratched them, and red-oak branches whacked them on the head. They tried to jump a gully and fell in; it was muddy in the bottom.

The girl suddenly burst into wild sobs.

"What's the matter?" Rush asked.

"Poor Uncle Jethro!" sobbed the girl.

Rush had temporarily forgotten Uncle Jethro, but now he remembered. That had been too bad. "Yes, it was sad," he agreed.

"He was such a nice old man to die," choked the girl.

"Very sad," agreed Rush.

"Yes." The girl sobbed some more. "But he was awful when he was dead. I mean—it was terrible being locked in there with his body."

"Yes, it—" Rush stopped. What? What did you say? Locked in there with his body?"

"Yes, locked in four days, while they tried to find someone to kill me."

"Great grief!" said Rush.

"Why are you so surprised?"

"Was that Uncle Jethro lying back there, shot between the eyes, in that box in the shack?" Rush asked.

"Yes, of course. Uncle Jethro."

"Uncle Jethro didn't get burned up in an automobile accident in New York?"

"No. He was shot in the woods."

"I am mystified," said Rush.

THE FARMER was waiting in the road in the Model T—he had lighted a ten-cent cigar and he was leaning back in the car seat, reading a copy of a well-known fifty-cent men's magazine, or at least looking at the pictures.

Said the farmer, "You must have done some powerful squirrel huntin' over in that brush, judgin' from the shootin'."

"Yes. It was powerful," Rush admitted.

"Get anything?"

"A headache."

They rode toward town.

Rush took an inventory of his feminine companion, and decided it was the most pleasant thing he had found to do so far. She was long, but not too long, with curves. She had hair of the color of good rich honey, and eyes of deep and entrancing midnight blue. Probably under other circumstances she wouldn't be quite so pale. She was nice.

"Name?" Rush asked.

"Annie," the girl said.

"You said Uncle Jethro was shot in the woods," Rush reminded her.

"Yes. Only not this woods. Another one, over toward Bear Creek. We were squirrel hunting. Uncle Jethro liked to hunt squirrels." She paused to wipe away an involuntary tear. "Uncle Jethro always said I made a noise and scared the squirrels, though. He made me stay back, while he went ahead."

The girl took a deep breath and wiped her eyes.

"On this occasion," she said, "Uncle Jethro had made me stay back and he had gone on ahead. He was out of sight. All of a sudden, he came running back. Uncle Jethro was excited. He said to me: 'Annie, I've found something awful bad. Come on. We've got to run.' And I asked, 'What for, Uncle Jethro?' Uncle Jethro said, 'Run for your life!' Well, we ran, but pretty soon a man—it was that Slim—jumped out of the brush and shot Uncle Jethro between the eyes."

"Slim shot Uncle Jethro between the eyes," Rush muttered.

"And Uncle Jethro fell dead. Then Slim pointed his gun at me. But he… he… he couldn't shoot. He couldn't kill a girl. So they took me to that shack. And ever since, they have been telling me that they had sent to the city for a professional killer to come up and put me out of the way."

"What did Uncle Jethro find in the woods?" asked Rush.

"I have no idea."

"Whatever it was, it made those men kill him?"

"Yes."

"I am still mystified," Rush said.

The Model T reached paved highway U.S. 63, and Rush expected it to turn south. Instead, it turned north.

"Hey," said Rush, "haven't you got your directions mixed, Mr. Farmer?"

"Not me," said the farmer. "I ain't deaf. I heard what was just said. I'm taking you-all to the sheriff. I'm one of his deputies."

THE MODEL T ran with a great deal of noise, the farmer steering with both arms; occasionally the engine missed on one cylinder, and at intervals on at least three cylinders at once, at which times it gave a terrific jackrabbit jump.

Uncle Jethro's bones rattled in the tin box.

One of the jumps of the car caused Rush's suitcase containing the toad to fall open, revealing the toad.

"What is that?" asked the girl.

"A toad."

"Why do you carry such a thing around?" inquired the girl.

"To get mad at," Rush said. He put the toad back and closed the suitcase.

The sheriff looked as if he knew his job. He gave his deputy a ten-cent cigar and dusted off chairs for them to sit in.

"You all look excited," he said, "so let's have a simple story of your troubles."

The girl told the same story she had given Rush in the car. It was identical, almost word for word, about how Uncle Jethro had found something in the woods and been shot because of it. She painted a very grisly picture of how she had been held in the shack with the corpse while the men hunted for someone with low enough scruples to kill a woman.

She turned and pointed at Rush.

"They found him," she said. "There he is."

"*What?*" yelled Rush.

"Oh, you haven't fooled me a bit," the girl said. "You are a hired killer they brought to the shack. You fell out with them. Probably you decided you weren't getting enough money for killing me. You ran Slim and the others away. You then tried to deceive me into thinking you were a lily-white fellow."

"You're under arrest," the sheriff told Rush.

"But—"

"And the best thing for you to do," added the sheriff, "is to tell us what Uncle Jethro found in the woods that made your friends kill him."

"But—"

"Tell!" yelled the sheriff. "Tell all!"

"But—"

"Get the rubber hose," Roared the sheriff. "We'll beat the truth out of him."

CHAPTER IV

ON BEAR CREEK

IT LOOKED VERY bad, there was no doubt, and Rush did not blame them, either, nor did he want to tell the story of Uncle Jethro and the will, because that was a crack-brained matter that doubtless would not be believed. Still, he had no other story to tell, and he needed one badly, so might as well out with that one.

"It began," he said, "with Uncle Jethro—"

"Don't let him fool you, sheriff!" cried the girl. "Don't let him! I know all about that Uncle Jethro business he will tell you."

"What do you know about it?" asked Rush curiously.

"Why, when those men were trying to hire a killer, they telephoned the city, and they used a false name. They used Uncle Jethro's name. They told the city gangsters they were contacting that Uncle Jethro wanted to hire a man to kill a girl. They thought it was a good joke to use Uncle Jethro's name. Because Uncle Jethro was already dead."

"I see," Rush said.

He didn't see anything.

Except one thing. He'd better get out of here. This sheriff meant business, and they might even electrocute him before they got done, because Slim and the others were convinced he was a hired killer, too.

Rush crossed his legs and took hold of the heel of his left shoe.

"Wait!" growled the sheriff. "What're you doing?"

"The heel is loose on my shoe," Rush said.

The heel wasn't very loose. He had to give it quite a tug. Then he tossed it out on the floor, in front of the door.

"Look at that!" he exclaimed.

They looked. Rush didn't. He turned his head quickly. The heel suddenly burst into blue-hot flame. It made a light like an electric arc welder; it was absolutely impossible to look at that light.

Everyone there was momentarily blinded. But not for long. They had only to look away, and their eyes would recover.

Rush acted. He jumped, grabbed the girl. He carried her in his arms and sprang over the blazing chemical—a compound that was a variation of thermite, with which he had experimented a great deal—in the shoe heel.

He had tossed the thing conveniently in front of the door for a good reason. It was blazing higher. It would blaze still higher; in fact, it would fill the whole doorway with a sheet of blue-hot flame in a moment.

Rush sprang out into the corridor with the girl. The flame rushed up, and prevented the sheriff following him. The sheriff began to shoot off a gun.

Rush ran out of the courthouse, which contained the sheriff's office.

In front of the courthouse stood the car used by the State highway patrolman assigned to that section. Rush started to run the other direction, then realized the patrolman was not in his car.

Rush borrowed the State highway patrol car. It was not locked, of course; the cops in New York City are the only ones who feel it necessary to lock their own cars.

It was a good car. When they turned south on U.S. Highway 63, Rush got it up to ninety miles an hour, just to see what it would do if he had to. He slowed down.

"Do you know what I'm going to do now?" he asked the girl.

She had tried kicking him on the shins, gouging him in the eyes, and pulling his hair. He had managed to survive that.

"You haven't any choice," she said. "You'll have to kill me."

RUSH TURNED left off the highway, on dirt road, then asked a question. "Where is Bear Creek?" he demanded.

The girl pressed her lips together stubbornly.

"Listen," said Rush, "I don't see what you've got to gain by being a Miss Sphinx."

"You've got no choice, but to kill me," the girl said.

"Do you want to die right now?" Rush asked. "Or would you care to answer questions and take a chance on persuading me not to behave as you think I'm going to."

"It depends on what you want to know," the girl decided.

"Where is Bear Creek?"

"You're headed toward it."

"Where is the woods where Uncle Jethro got shot?"

"You turn south the next mile, then go on east."

"Thank you," said Rush.

After that, he did not do much but drive, which was enough. The road had only one good quality; it was straight. Some of the culverts were half washed out, and the road did not look as if the farmers had dragged it in a year, because the ruts seemed to average a foot deep. They began to enter hills and woods.

"Close?" asked Rush.

"About half a mile."

"Near enough," Rush said.

He got out of the car, navigating a little lopsidedly because of the heel missing from his left shoe, and dropped the young woman a courtesy.

"Goodbye," he said.

She paled. "You're—you're—"

"Turning you loose," Rush said. "You can go back. You can stay here. You can do whatever you please. Except that you had better not follow me into this brush."

"Better not follow. What are you going to do?"

"You remember that Uncle Jethro found something in the woods?" Rush asked.

"Yes."

"Well, it may still be there. I'm going to look. Those men, Slim and the others, may have rushed back to move whatever it was."

The girl passed a hand over her brow. She seemed dazed. "You're going to let me go," she said, "if I want to go."

Rush nodded. "Goodbye," he said. "Put a good word for me in with the sheriff, if you see him."

THE WOODS were thick, composed of great walnut, hickory and elm trees, with a dense undergrowth of scrub oaks and buckbrush. There were squirrel nests in the trees, but no squirrels. Rush listened. There was no sound of the girl leaving, so he crept back and looked.

She was sitting there in the car.

While Rush was watching, she got out of the car and crossed to the other side of the road and concealed herself behind-some wild grapevines that draped heavily over the fence.

Rush resumed his hunt.

His goal turned out to be an old shed of slabs. It appeared there had once been a sawmill at the spot, and the old slab shed was all that was left. It was a very sturdy shed, for all its dilapidated looks.

In front of the shed stood a truck, a big farm stock truck, the bed ordinarily covered by a canvas; but the canvas cover now lay on the ground beside the truck. The engine was running.

It was the running engine that had made the finding easy for Rush.

Slim came out of the shed with a bundle done up in gunny-sacking, and threw the bundle in the truck. A moment later, the short man in coveralls also came out with a bundle which he dumped in the truck. Then bush jacket. They went back for more.

They were in a hurry.

CHAPTER V
THE SKIN GAME

RUSH TOOK THE heel off his other shoe. This contained smoke bombs. Smoke bombs were not a very effective weapon, but it was all he had left. He had not arrived on the scene equipped with his usual array of gadgets, and accordingly he had only such of them as he had been wearing by accident.

The smoke bombs were about the size of pigeon eggs—Rush's shoes had rather high heels, to make room—and they were fitted with little firing levers which had to be thrown with a fingernail, although, like a grenade, the firing levers could be held down by a finger as long as they were retained in the hand. Rush got all of the smoke bombs ready to detonate, held them in his hand, and walked to the shed.

The shed had a peculiar odor. A very strong odor. He noticed that, and also the fact that the smell was familiar, even if it was one that wasn't found around a city very often.

Rush tossed all bombs inside. He waited. A split-second later, they all opened, sounding as if someone had dropped a hatful of rotten eggs.

The shed had a heavy door that could be hasped fast on the inside. Rush went into the shed, pulled the door, shut, and fastened it.

He began finding people in the dark and hitting them. The smoke was behaving very effectively—the inside of the shed was the darkest place Rush had ever seen. He found one man; he touched the fellow's arm.

"*Sh-h-h!*" Rush breathed in the fellow's ear. "Stand still."

The man thought it was one of his consorts, so he stood still, and made a nice stationary target. There was a loud smack of a report, and Rush's right arm tingled all the way to the elbow.

"What the hell?" yelled Slim's voice. "What made this smoke?"

"*Sh-h-h!*" Rush said. "There's a firebug in here."

He walked toward Slim's voice, but bumped into someone, and whoever it was knocked him down. Rush fell over a pile of the bundles that he had noticed them loading in the truck. He picked up one of the burlap-swathed bundles, hurled it. He missed. He missed with several more bundles, and at the bottom of the pile, he found some heavy slabs that made a platform on which the bundles had been piled.

Rush picked up one of the slabs, walked around, and swung the slab like a broadsword. It made hissing noises. It did not hit anybody.

There had been some yelling and profanity.

Men began beating the door. Rush ran over, set himself with his improvised broadsword, and mowed one man down, and badly jarred another. The jarred one was Slim. He sprang upon Rush.

Slim was the last of them, but he was enough. He wrapped Rush with his legs, and held on. He swung his fists. He seemed to have a good deal of luck—they could not see each other in the intense darkness, but Slim seemed to connect with every punch, while Rush missed most of his.

Rush finally got up dizzily and ran, with Slim's legs wrapped around his waist, into the side of the shed. Slim's head crashed into the slabs, and he came loose. Rush got on him and pounded with both fists.

It was quiet for a few moments.

Then a stick beat on the door.

"It's the sheriff!" cried the girl's voice. "Come out with your hands up!"

"I know it's not the sheriff," said Rush. "He couldn't get here this quick. But you better go get him."

"Are you all right?"

"Do you care?"

"Sure," said the girl. "I rather liked you all along."

THE SHERIFF, later in the afternoon, came into his office from the direction of the jail. He hooked his thumbs in his suspenders. His deputy gave out ten-cent cigars.

"Minks and weasels and things," he said. "Furs. Foxes and skunks and wolves and muskrats and raccoons."

"That shed was almost full." Rush said.

"Sure. Almost forty thousand dollars' worth of skins."

"What was forty thousand dollars' worth of furs doing in that shed in the woods on Bear Creek?" asked Rush.

"Stolen. We had a big fur robbery here last spring, about the end of the trapping season. Feller buys hides from farmers and trappers all over this end of Missouri, besides Iowa and Illinois. Kept 'em in a building until the buyers could come around from the city. One night, thieves tied up the guards and took three truckloads of his best stuff."

"Uncle Jethro found where they had 'em hid. They killed Uncle Jethro," put in the deputy.

"Minks and weasels, eh?" said Rush.

"Well, minks, anyway. When I said weasels, I was referrin' to the thieves. Weasels ain't considered fur-bearin' varmints in this neck of the woods."

Rush said, "How about taking these handcuffs off me?"

"Sure. Forgot to tell you. That Slim confessed."

Rush rubbed his wrists. Then he went to his suitcase, which stood in the sheriff's office, and opened it and took out the toad. He set the toad on the sheriff's desk. There was a desk light on the table, and Rush removed the shade, then switched this on, and stuck the lighted bulb in the toad's mouth.

"What in tarnation you doin?" the sheriff demanded.

"I have a terrible suspicion," Rush said.

There was a click from the toad, then a humming. This indicated the heat of the light bulb had caused the thermostat inside the thing to turn on the wired wireless "transceiver" so that communication was now possible—providing there was a similar "transceiver" in operation somewhere in the city.

"Hello," Rush said, close to the ear of the toad.

"Heh, heh," said the toad. *"How did you like it?"*

Rush turned purple. He started to say some things, but realized a girl was present.

"So you framed me again!" he snarled to the toad. "That Uncle Jethro in New York was some ham actor you hired. The whole thing was a hooligan you worked on me. What about those bones in the burned car in New York?"

"Soup bones," said the voice of Bufa, the toad, *"obtainable at any butcher shop."*

Rush glared. "And how did you get track of the whole mystery?" He thought of something. "Say—did you—the city gangsters Slim contacted to kill the girl didn't—"

"Yep," said Bufa. *"I have my contacts for locating unusual crimes. The man Slim called happened to be one. We arranged the rest."*

Rush was so enraged he couldn't think of anything to say. But wait! Damn yes! One thing.

"What about my ten thousand dollars for solving an unusual crime?" he shouted.

"Uncle Jethro's will."

"What?"

There was no sound from the toad. The apparatus was dead. The other "transceiver" had been switched off. The mysterious voice of Bufa, the toad, the voice of some person unknown who had almost a maniacal desire to see unusual crimes solved, was through speaking.

Rush said, "Uncle Jethro's will, Uncle Jethro's will—"

He dived to the sheriff's desk and scooped up the picture frame. He broke the glass with the barrel of the sheriff's pistol.

Under the note that bore Uncle Jethro's will, there reposed a ten-thousand-dollar bank note.

"Excuse me," Rush said. He went out and walked around until he found an empty room in the courthouse. He entered and closed the door. He swore until he was out of breath.

He went back into the sheriff's office.

"I feel terrible," he said.

"We'll have to cheer you up," said the girl.

Rush had been thinking that she might be able to do that, too.

THE REMARKABLE ZEKE

THE REMARKABLE ZEKE WAS
SIMPLY STUPENDOUS WHEN IT
CAME TO KILLING FOLKS!

CHAPTER I

DEATH OF A BULLFROG

FOR SOMEONE WHO had received a gift through the mail, the man with the black eye behaved strangely.

The man was wearing colored glasses, obviously to hide his black eye, because when he carried the package from the parcel-post window to one of the writing desks in the post office, and pushed the dark glasses up on his forehead so that he could see to untie the string, the shiner became very noticeable.

Five feet five would catch his height, which meant he was about the height of the average woman, although there was nothing else feminine about him. He did not have two horns or a tail, but people frequently said, "There goes a bull." They didn't mean a policeman, either.

The package was small. It might have been a box of kitchen matches, done up in brown paper and a string. The man listened to it. He kept his ear very close to it for quite a while. Then he hefted it in his hands, judging its weight. He smirked.

His smirk indicated that he had decided conclusively that the packet was too light to hold a bomb.

The man opened the package. At once, he emitted a howl. It was a bawl-squall-bellow kind of a howl. It made a mail clerk drop a mailsack, and caused a Scotty dog that a woman was leading on a leash to run under a table and yowl as if he was being murdered.

The man continued to roar. He also made a wild pass at the package, and knocked it onto the floor. The paper and cardboard hit the floor, and a bullfrog hopped out.

The man stamped wildly at the frog.

The bullfrog was not large, as bullfrogs come. No epicure would glance at this one and visualize froglegs sauté. The frog had a starved look, and if anyone felt inclined to feel sorry for frogs, this one appeared to be a deserving subject for sympathy.

It turned out that there was another gentleman in the post office who could feel sorry for frogs.

"Here, here, you cruel rascal!" this man shouted.

He dashed forward. He was a long man, and he was as skinny as the frog. He was sheathed in a black suit, wore a stiff celluloid collar and a bow tie and a derby, and carried an umbrella. He was prissy.

"You can't do that!" he yelled.

The man with the black eye was doing it, anyway. He was stamping the frog. The frog was active and went hopping across the floor, but once he did not hop soon enough, and he became rather shapeless on the floor. The man with the black eye did some more stamping for good measure.

"You're under arrest, you cruel beast!" shouted the long prissy man.

"Who the hell," asked the man with the black eye, "might you be?"

"I am a member in good standing of the L.E.M.A." the other advised proudly. And added coldly, "It's too bad you do not have the good qualities of Zeke."

That explained it. Except, possibly, that there was no such thing as a member in good standing of the L.E.M.A., as far as the general public was concerned. They were all

a bunch of nannies. The L.E.M.A. was the League for Ending Mistreatment of Animals, and it had no connection, actual or implied, with the A.S.P.C.A., the American Society for the Prevention of Cruelty to Animals, of which everybody has heard, and which does a good work. The L.E.M.A. was strictly a gang of old goats and fanatics and busybodies. Worse, still, it liked to get its name in the newspapers.

There was a brief fight in the post office.

The bull-shaped man with the black eye was led off to jail.

The prissy L.E.M.A. member went to a hospital, whining that all his bones were broken. But first, he put the flattened carcass of the frog in a fruit jar and gave it to the police as evidence.

That evening, they brought supper to the man with the black eye. The jailer said, "Hey, buddy, the boys chipped in and bought you a bottle of domestic champagne. They like the job you done on the L.E.M.A."

No answer.

"What's wrong?" asked the jailer.

The prisoner was lying on his back, dead.

Now, all of this was very queer, of course.

CLICKELL RUSH, who frequently decided he didn't like being known as the Gadget Man, came out of the hotel dining room that evening with a full feeling and a tooth-pick.

Rush stopped at the hotel newsstand and said, "Are the morning papers out yet?"

The clerk behind the newsstand stared at Rush, then shook his head, and clucked *"Tsk, tsk!"* disapprovingly.

"As long as there is only one Zeke," he said, "you shouldn't be a detective."

"I'm not," Rush said.

"Oh, yes, you are. You're Clickell Rush, and you've made quite a hell of a name for yourself. It's a shame, too."

"Are the morning papers out yet?" Rush repeated.

"It's really a shame, about you being a detective," the clerk repeated sadly.

"On account of why?" Rush asked.

"I haven't any shoes on," said the clerk.

"You—what's the idea?"

"I'm going hunting. These are my stalking feet."

Rush looked intently at the newsstand clerk. He did not say anything.

"Well—laugh," said the clerk. "That was a gag. I'm learn-ing to be a radio gag man. Go ahead and laugh."

"It wasn't funny."

"My name is Oliver," the clerk said.

Oliver was not quite round, but if he happened to be running fast and stubbed his toe, he would doubtless roll over and over. He had freckles and a grin.

"You are a very happy-looking young man," Rush said, "so let's not forget ourselves and ruin each other's disposition. To avoid further such inclinations on our part, why not answer my question: Are the morning papers out yet?"

"Do you," asked Oliver, "light your cigars with your right hand?"

"Of course."

"Hmmm. Most people use a match."

A man came in from the street with an armload of the latest newspapers and slammed them down on the showcase. Rush took one, and counted out the three cents that it cost.

"I hardly believe you have a sense of humor," Oliver said regretfully.

"I don't quite make you out, Oliver," Rush said, and went upstairs to his room, where he found that someone had paid him a visit and opened his largest suitcase and taken Bufa out.

Bufa now sat on a typewritten note and one half of a ten-thousand-dollar bill.

Rush threw his newspaper down. Then he stood in the middle of the room and swore so loud and expressively that someone threw up a window somewhere and shouted, "Stop that language, my friend, unless you want me to call a cop!"

THE NOTE on which Bufa sat was short and simple. It said:

I WOULDST TALK TO YOU.

If the note had been a joke, it would have been mildly funny. But it wasn't a joke, so it was silly.

But not as silly as Bufa, the toad. Bufa was somewhat larger than a football, and had a green back, mud-yellow underside, and a wide-open mouth. Bufa, the toad, was too ugly to be a pleasant ornament, and the thing was not an ornament, anyway.

Bufa, the toad, contained a compact wired-radio "transceiver," an intricate assemblage of apparatus which made it possible to talk and hear over the lines of the city electric light system. Rush understood all about the entrails of Bufa.

Rush was a mechanical wizard—not a detective. That is, he had been trying for some time not to be a detective. It was a little difficult.

Some months before, Rush had taken several thousand gadgets and ideas which he had invented for catching crooks, and brought them to New York City, where he had hoped to sell them to the police department. He had been thoroughly laughed at. The newspaper reporters had written funny stories, and the public had laughed, too; It was kind of whacky.

Then one day Rush found Bufa, the toad, in his room, and Bufa was sitting on a note and one half of a ten-thousand-dollar bill. The note told Rush how to tune the toad in—put a lighted electric light bulb in the thing's gaping mouth, so the bulb's warmth would close a thermostat which in turn would switch on the self-contained "transceiver" inside the toad—and Rush had obeyed instructions.

A voice came from Bufa and instructed Rush to solve a mysterious crime, and he would get the other half of the ten-thousand-dollar bill. Rush had done so. He needed the ten thousand, which he received.

But it hadn't ended there. Rush had to keep on solving unusual crimes. Whenever he refused, he found himself skillfully involved, so that he had to be a detective, whether he wished or not.

Rush still had no idea who the voice of Bufa might be.

It was all incredible, and so it was silly. The whole thing quite silly—except the half of a ten-thousand-dollar bill. There is something about such a bill, or even half of one.

A whole roomful of people can be laughing hilariously, but let someone produce a ten-thousand-dollar bill, and the laughter will instantly stop. There is undeniably something about such a bill.

Unfortunately, Rush needed ten thousand very badly at the moment. He had just finished backing one of his own inventions, and it had been a thorough flop. Maybe he was cut out to be a gadget detective, after all.

He put Bufa, the toad, into operation.

"Hello," he said, "what kind of a madman's holiday have you got in mind this time?"

Bufa, the toad, said, *"Read in the newspaper about the poor frog that got stepped on, then look into it."*

That was all. Just one sentence. Unusual, for the voice of Bufa, since the mysterious individual, whoever he or she was, usually liked to kid around and say stuff about being "Bufa, of the species *Bufonidæ,* feeding upon slugs and snails, human variety."

This time, the voice of Bufa sounded as if it had been disguised by talking against a piece of paper which was in turn held against an ordinary comb. The voice had a comb-music quality, it seemed to Rush.

RUSH WENT through the hotel lobby in a hurry, but Oliver, the newsman, hailed him anyway.

"If a little imp lost his tail," said Oliver, "where could he go to have the mishap repaired?"

"Search me," Rush said.

"Why not a bootlegger?" asked Oliver. "That's where bad spirits are retailed."

"That's not funny," Rush said.

"I'll bet Zeke would think it was funny," Oliver said. "I'll be a radio gag man yet. You watch me!"

CHAPTER II

TWO DEAD

THE ATTITUDE OF the police was best described by that phrase in use among social matrons—barely polite.

The night desk sergeant made a little speech. He said, "I hoped, damn me to the hot place, that we would never see your face around here, Mr. Clickell Rush. However, I see there is no such fortune, so what is the use of going into that? Anyway, the man is dead."

Rush said, "I know the man is dead. He stamped on a frog that he got in a box through the mail, and then a L.E.M.A. busybody had him arrested, and then he died in his cell. It was all in the newspapers."

"Then what do you want?"

"I want to see him."

"You don't look, Mr. Rush, like the kind of a man who has fun by going around looking at dead ones."

"I'm not a very humorous fellow," Rush suggested. "I just want to look at the body."

"Have you got a private detective's license?"

"I haven't got a license to hunt, fish, marry, or own a dog. You don't have to be licensed to have a curiosity, do you?"

"I give up," the desk sergeant said.

Clickell Rush was not a large man, but nature had fitted him with a remarkable set of sinews, a sample of which stood out like fountain pens on the backs of his hands when he tightened his fingers. The muscles were the more remarkable, since he took very little exercise, only what he had to. He did not like exercise any more than he liked being a detective. He did like brown suits—and brown neckties, brown socks, brown shirts, brown hats, brown shoes, brown gloves and brown handkerchiefs to go with the brown suits. He always wore some shade of brown in everything.

Rush was wiping his face with a brown handkerchief when he came out of the police morgue. He was pale. He had just disgraced himself by being sick.

"Well, you asked for it," said the desk sergeant, who had let a patrolman sit in his place and come along.

"B-but they were shooting craps in there," Rush said in an ill voice, "and bouncing the dice against one of the *bodies*. It made me—*ugh!*"

"Yep, it made you *ugh!* all right." The cop chuckled. "Howsoever I wouldn't feel so bad. They were kinda laying it on in there for your benefit, only don't tell them I told you so."

"Why lay it on for me?" Rush asked dully.

"Well, heck! You're a famous private detective."

"I am, eh?"

"Yeah, and a famous private detective is a cop's idea of a Gargantuan sample of equine posterior, if you get what I mean."

"You are very frank. Thank you."

"The deceased was named Harold Schraft. His occupation was raising pickles, or cucumbers, whichever you want to call them. Cucumbers before and pickles after, I guess. Anyway, he had a farm outside of town about five miles, down by the river. Lived alone. No enemies, No friends. No money to speak of."

"Why was Harold Schraft scared of frogs?"

"Huh?"

"As soon as he saw the frog in the post office, he yelled and howled and stamped on the frog."

"Yeah. That's right."

RUSH HEARD THE VOICE OF TWO MEN—AND A DOG BARKED.

"Could he have been scared of frogs, and so shocked by seeing a frog that his heart failed him or something?"

"The chemist and the doctors ain't figured what killed him, yet. But it wasn't his heart. We don't know yet for sure what it was, but Harold Schraft didn't die from being scared by no frog."

"What is the L.E.M.A. busy-body's name, and where does he live?"

"His name is Shamus O'Leary. 14-20 West Street."

Rush walked out of the police station and reached the sidewalk, and an elderly coupé drew up to the curb and stopped, and a round head thrust out the window to ask, "Give you a lift, Mr. Rush?"

"Why, Oliver!" Rush said.

"I WAS just driving by," Oliver explained, "and thinking about appetite."

"Appetite?"

"When you're eating, you're 'appy, and when you get done you're tight. Such is appetite. A gag. Get it?"

"Oliver," Rush said patiently, "you weren't following me, by any chance?"

"Me?" said Oliver. "Oh, my goodness!"

"Very well," Rush said. "A man stamped on a frog in the post office this afternoon, and another man had him arrested. We are going to see the man who had the arresting done. His name is Shamus O'Leary."

"Shamus O'Leary doesn't sound like a name that would fit him."

"No, it doesn't," Rush admitted.

"Why are you interested in Shamus O'Leary?"

"Let me tell you the secret of successful detecting, Oliver. I read it in a recent book by a very famous and efficient detective named Ricky Rivers, and it was so good it stuck in my mind. This Ricky Rivers is a very skillful sleuth, and some day I must meet him. However, the morsel was this: You follow up all the angles, Oliver, even if there are ten thousand, because the ten thousandth one may lead to the solution."

"Thank you," Oliver said. "I believe I could apply the same idea to my ambition to be a radio gag man."

"Oliver," said Rush gently, "why do you suppose I am talking to you so much, if not to keep you from thinking of any more of those terrible jokes."

"I have named this car Baby," Oliver said.

"Why?"

"Because it doesn't go anywhere without its rattle."

Rush maintained an appropriately cool silence during the remainder of the ride.

HE GOT to thinking, and it occurred to him that another one of his vacations seemed to have blown up. He had come to this town, Tulsa, Oklahoma, because he had visited it once before, and its clean buildings—they burned natural gas here, so there was no smoke—had appealed to him. He had thought he would do some deep thinking, and get himself straightened out. He was still convinced he was an inventor, but he couldn't seem to invent anything that people didn't think was somewhat zany. So he had come to Tulsa three days ago, and after he had a good rest, he had planned to walk along the sandy bed of the Arkansas River and throw rocks in the water, or maybe go up to Spavinaw Lake and catch a fish. But here his vacation had turned into another one of the utterly wild-eyed things, one of the unusual crimes which Bufa wanted him to solve.

He wondered how Bufa kept track of him. He wondered who the voice of Bufa could be, and how the owner of the voice managed to keep out of an institution for mental cases. If this sort of thing kept up, Rush wondered how *he* was going to keep out of an institution.

At Shamus O'Leary's home, a white house that was neat and conservative, they found a hearse just backing up to the front door. They were taking an empty coffin out of the hearse.

"What has happened?" Rush asked.

"Why," said the undertaker, "poor Mr. Shamus O'Leary has passed on. Right after dinner tonight, he had a heart attack, and was with us only a short time after that."

"Have you called the police?" asked Rush.

"Why, no."

"I would," Rush said, "and I would also call a better doctor."

WHEN THEY returned to the police station, and parked in front of the door, a newsboy rushed up to them, flourished his papers and yelled, "Read all about Zeke! Buy a paper, mister!"

Rush went into the police station and Oliver followed him. Rush turned around and asked, "What does this mean, Oliver?"

Oliver looked around in surprise. "Why, I was thinking up a gag, and I guess I just absent-mindedly followed you in here."

Rush went over and talked to the desk sergeant, who was wearing a bewildered look and writing reports in his book.

"Have the chemists or the doctors found out what they died of?" Rush asked.

"No." The desk sergeant rubbed his jaw. "You know, this is becoming slightly strange. I would hate to think those two men were murdered, and I wanted to ask you about that. If you was me, would you think they had been murdered?"

"I thought," Rush said, "that the general cop opinion of private detectives was a very low one."

"It is. I'll probably think the opposite of what you tell me."

Rush was thoughtful for some moments. "What about that black eye?"

"Eh?"

"The black eye that the man had before he got the frog through the mail. Was anything done about that?"

"Questions were asked, but he just said he bumped into a door."

"And the frog?"

"Oh, the frog. Well, we've got it here in a fruit jar. The L.E.M.A. man wanted it for evidence in court in the morning, but I guess it won't make much difference to him, now that he's dead."

"Could I have it?"

"What the hell you want with a mashed frog?"

"I don't know. I just want it."

"Well, you can't—hmmm—why not? What's the difference? However, we might want it back."

"I'll do my best to take good care of it."

Rush was given the frog, which was contained in a Mason fruit jar. At first glance, the remains in the fruit jar bore little resemblance to a frog, but close inspection indicated it was.

"Where are the wrappings the frog came in?" Rush asked.

"The wrapping? Why, heck, nobody thought to get them! This thing was just a fight between a L.E.M.A. man and a fellow who had stamped on a frog, when it started."

Rush said, "Well, thank you," and turned to leave, carrying the fruit jar containing the remains. He bumped into Oliver.

"You still here?" Rush said.

Oliver said, "I get jittery from thinking of the two hidden skeletons."

"Hidden where?"

"Inside us. That's the gag I was thinking up. Nifty, eh?"

Rush walked out of the police station and Oliver trailed him. Oliver ran ahead and opened the coupé door. They got in, drove slowly, and in the middle of the fourth block a gray sedan stopped suddenly ahead of them—halted so unexpectedly that Oliver bumped the other car lightly.

"Gosh, I'm sorry!" Oliver said. "I was thinking what a swell gag that was."

Two men got out of the gray sedan, one alighting from either side, and came back and examined their bumper to see what damage had been done. None had been done. Both men grinned, then walked to Oliver's car, as if they intended to apologize to Rush and Oliver for stopping so suddenly. But instead of apologizing, they wrenched open the coupé doors and showed Rush and Oliver the business ends of large dark-blue revolvers.

CHAPTER III

ZEKE

RUSH SAID, "OLIVER, I guess it was a mistake for you to offer me a ride."

It was as dark on the street as it could be with a street light at each end of the block, and there were a few overhanging trees, no lights in the houses. There was almost no traffic in sight; just one car which rolled up slowly and stopped, while the driver stuck out his head and rubbered, thinking there had been an accident. He saw no damage, probably concluded it was just some friends picking an unusual place to talk, and drove on. The two men with the guns had kept very still while the motorist paused.

There was some vague resemblance about them, although they were not of the same size or of similar coloring. One was a redhead, blue-eyed and freckled and pugnacious. The other was a little man with swarthy skin and piercing dark eyes. But both of them had rather bovine faces, and neither was exactly thin. It was probably this bull-solid build that gave an impression that they had something in common.

Rush said, "Harold Schraft was built something like a bull, too," thoughtfully.

"What's that?" one of them asked.

"Harold Schraft—the man who got a frog through the mail, then died."

The pair glanced at each other. They were uneasy. But their guns, which showed in the glow from the dashlight, were steady.

"I believe you're right," one said to the other. "He's pretty slick. He sees through things."

The other nodded. "Yes, I had read about him. I knew he had some pretty fair wits. I figured right from the first he was as good as Zeke."

"As good as Zeke? You think so?"

"Well, you don't get a reputation in newspapers by sitting in a rocking chair."

"But Zeke—he may not be able to handle Zeke."

"We can throw him in there and let him try."

"Because of one reason and another," Rush remarked, "I am beginning to notice the name of Zeke cropping up frequently."

"Get your car over to the curb and leave it," ordered one of the ox-bodied men. "Then get in the back seat of our heap."

"When you use the word 'heap,'" said Oliver, "I presume you are employing a colloquialism for the word automobile?"

"We got two humorists with us," one bullish man growled.

"Only one," Rush said. "Count me out."

They parked Oliver's car, then entered the gray sedan. The sedan was a long machine with a small folding seat on which one of the thick men could sit and face them with his revolver. He did not hold the revolver openly, but tossed a laprobe over the gun. They rolled east on Eleventh Street to Peoria.

Oliver nudged Rush and said disgustedly, "Why don't you do something? I thought you were the famous gadget-man detective, with a gadget for every emergency."

"What makes you think this is an emergency?" Rush asked.

At the intersection of Peoria and Fifteenth, they stopped for a red light, and a newsboy ambled out to the car and shouted, "Late paper! Read all about Zeke!"

"No, thanks, son," one of the thick men said.

The sedan moved on down a slight grade, and they turned left into a section where the houses were increasingly splendid and surrounded by grounds as large as pastures. Near one of these imposing mansions, the car stopped.

"Got the stuff you took out of the post-office wastebasket?" asked one stocky man.

"Yep," said his partner.

"You want me to do the next part of the little job?"

"You might as well."

The man sitting in front of Rush pointed at the great house, in which a few windows were lighted, and said, "You see that little hut?"

Rush looked, and immediately knew he had made a mistake, but it was too late to do anything about it, although he tried to dodge anyway. He was unsuccessful, and the man's gun, swinging hard, hit him on the head, causing everything to become black.

PROBABLY RUSH was not out long, because his ears rang all the while, and were still ringing when he heard voices. They were the voices of two strange men, and a dog barked. The dog sounded like a large one.

"The dog smells something over this way," one voice stated.

"Yeah, I thought the noise was over that way, myself. It sounded like somebody fell off the wall."

Rush decided he was lying in some bushes—flowering bushes, from the smell of them—and that a high stone wall was at his back. In addition to the ache in his head and the ringing in his ears, both his hands and one leg seemed to be gashed slightly.

There was no sign of Oliver.

The dog was barking furiously in his face, and a flash-light was blinding him.

"See how his hands and leg are cut," one of the voices growled. "He fell off the wall. There's broken glass on top of that wall."

"Fell off and knocked himself dopey. Sure."

"We better take him to Zeke."

They took him to a great house which had a door manned by a butler. They put him in a chair in an all-mahogany room. The chair was enormous, and there were other huge chairs in the room, one of them occupied by a girl.

The two men who had found Rush—obviously they were private guards of the estate—explained that they had heard a noise and investigated and found Rush.

"Go away and let Zeke talk to him," the girl said.

The two private guards went out.

Rush did not say anything. The girl did not say anything. The room was very cool with air from a conditioning plant, that came out of a grating with a sound like a steady, gentle wind.

The girl was no extreme beauty, Rush decided, then changed his mind. She was all right. She was wholesome, and looked as if she laughed a lot. She was smiling faintly at him now. She wore gray tweeds and a green blouse and green pumps. Of all colors, Rush detested green most. That was why he had first thought she wasn't pretty.

"The burglary business has its ups and downs, doesn't it?" the girl remarked.

"Yes, it does," Rush admitted.

"Do you make much out of it, as a general rule?"

"Oh, sure," Rush said. "As much as thirty-five dollars a week. At least, I put it down as that much on my income tax. Didn't want to get in trouble, you know."

"No," the girl admitted. "You can't fool around with the income-tax people."

"Are you Zeke?"

"No. I'm Thelma."

Rush's head had about cleared. He felt over himself for damages, and came across a crinkling sound in one of his pockets. He pulled out a wad of paper and cardboard, which he opened up. It was just brown paper and cardboard, and a piece of string.

"Now what about this?" he asked, exhibiting the paper and cardboard.

He knew what it was—the cardboard had been the box that contained the frog, and the paper had been the wrapper. It was not exactly a guess, for Harold Schraft's name and a general delivery address were on the paper. Furthermore, the two blocky men in the gray sedan had mentioned getting something out of the wastebasket in the post office. What Rush wanted to know was why the paper and wrapper happened to be in his pocket.

"This stuff," Rush explained, "was around a frog."

The words aroused a man whom Rush had not noticed. The man got up from a chair which was facing the fireplace on the other side of the room.

The man was a strikingly small and ancient runt who wore a pair of dilapidated cowboy boots and an equally dilapidated cowboy hat. He came forward.

"This is Zeke," the girl explained.

ZEKE PUT two wrinkled knots of fists on his hips and scowled at Rush. In the past, Zeke had been a very wide, thick, ox-bodied man, Rush decided, but now he was getting old.

"Just who are you," Zeke asked, "and what are you doing here?"

There was something familiar about his voice. Rush stared at him, and after a moment, he got it. Zeke's voice somewhat resembled the voices of the two thick men in the gray sedan. And they in turn had resembled, in thickness at least, the man named Harold Schraft, who had received a frog in the mail, then died.

"Have you got brothers?" Rush asked.

"After seeing me, my old man would have drowned 'em. No."

Zeke jerked the brown wrapping paper and cardboard out of Rush's hands and examined it, then shook his head slowly and gave the stuff back to Rush.

"That was around a frog, eh?" Zeke said. "Well, what if it was?"

"A man named Harold Schraft died after he got the frog," Rush explained. "And so did a L.E.M.A. meddler named Shamus O'Leary, although I think *his* death was merely an accident."

Rush was watching both the withered old man and the girl as he spoke, but they did not show any particular emotion.

"Why tell us such stuff?" Zeke asked.

"Well, we just got to discussing this paper and cardboard."

"Humph."

"And besides, two fellows brought me here and sort of threw me over the wall to make your acquaintance."

"Two fellows?" Zeke did not sound at all interested. "What did they look like?"

Rush said pointedly, "They were thick like you, and somehow their voices sounded kind of like yours."

"That's ridiculous," the girl said. "You're an orphan, aren't you, Zeke? And you've always been a bachelor."

"Ha, ha," Zeke chortled. "Sure. I was an orphan, then a bachelor." He took a pipe out of his pocket, felt through his clothing. "And I'm out of tobacco."

He walked out of the room, and they could hear him growling loudly at the servants, demanding to know what had become of his tobacco.

"Then you're not his daughter?" Rush said.

"One of Zeke's oil derricks fell on my father when I was a baby," the girl explained. "Zeke raised me."

"Just who is Zeke?"

Zeke came back into the room, walking with bowlegged majesty, holding a lighted match over his pipe bowl and puffing out clouds of smoke that smelled like the result of old rags burning.

"He wants to know who you are, Zeke," the girl said.

"Hell, I'll tell him!" Zeke grinned. "I'm my own favorite subject."

ZEKE STOOD in the middle of the floor and bragged. He wore a big grin while he boasted, and his boasting wasn't disgusting. Instead, it was impressive.

This little man was wildcat king of the oil industry. He was the incredibly lucky Zeke Gilstrap, and for almost twenty years he had been going out in the most unlikely places and drilling oil wells and bringing in gushers. He had the Midas touch, and he also had more millions of dollars than the average man has dollars.

"I'm so rich," said Zeke, "that only my lawyers know how rich."

Rush discovered that the boasting could soon become tiresome, particularly when he got to thinking about the state of his own finances, which consisted almost entirely of the torn half of a ten-thousand-dollar bill.

"Your name seems to be a byword around this town," he said. "Why?"

"I'm giving away all my money," Zeke said cheerfully.

"*What?*"

"Today, I gave sixty million dollars to build a cancer hospital and operate it free of charge for twenty years," Zeke explained. "Was that in the newspapers?"

"I don't know."

"Sure it was. I'll show you."

Zeke proudly dragged out a newspaper. He had a stack of them. The headline on this one said:

ZEKE GIVES SIXTY MILLION FOR HOSPITALS.

"You see," Zeke said. "I'm getting famous."

"But will your money hold out?" Rush asked curiously.

"Hell, if I don't worry about that, why should anybody else?"

Rush stood up and said, "Well, I had better be going."

Zeke also stood up, and took a flat gold-inlaid and silver-plated automatic out of his clothing. It was an unusual weapon for anyone dressed as Zeke, in the traditional fashion of the Old West. He pointed the ornate pistol at Rush. "Yes," he said. "You had better be going. Only I will go along, to make sure that you won't get lost on your way to the police station."

"Zeke!" the girl said sharply.

"Sure, Thelma. He had a nice line of talk, but he's still a burglar."

"But he looks honest," Thelma insisted.

"When they look honest, watch out for 'em," Zeke advised her. "If you're a good girl, I'll take you down to the penitentiary to see him sometime."

CHAPTER IV

THE ANGRY HEIRS

RUSH WALKED OUT of the great house, the butler at the door giving him a frown as he left, and Zeke walking close on his heels, but not close enough to be knocked down if Rush decided to whirl suddenly and swing a fist.

Floodlights had been switched on, and the grounds of the great estate were aglow with soft light. They walked down a lane between tall pines, until the two estate guards came out of the shrubbery.

The two guards had three prisoners.

"We found these parked in a car in the side street," one guard said. "We listened to them, and kind of got the idea this burglar was a friend of theirs."

Rush examined the three captives, who were Oliver and the two chunky men. They appeared to have been shoved around and scuffed up slightly.

Oliver snapped, "You can't arrest us. Private guards have no right—"

"We also have deputy sheriff commissions," growled one estate guard, "so shut up."

Zeke chuckled grimly. "Have you some handcuffs?"

"I'll get some out of my room over the garage," said a guard. "I have just enough to go around and one to spare."

The girl came along when they brought the handcuffs back.

After they were handcuffed together—Rush, Oliver and the two solid men—Zeke dismissed his guards, saying, "Thelma and me will take them down to the police station by ourselves."

"But Mr. Zeke! Four against two—"

"Don't insult me!" Zeke barked. "Go on back to your guarding. And give me that spare handcuff."

They were made to walk back to the gray sedan, and climb into the back seat.

Zeke searched them. He made a mound on the front seat of the stuff he removed from Rush's pockets and clothing.

"What is this junk?" Zeke asked.

"Gadgets," Rush explained.

Zeke picked up a small flat case which held a powerful amplifier using vacuum tubes, a device which Rush could connect to a microphone—the mike was in the pile of articles, too—and eavesdrop. Zeke did not appear to know what the thing was. He scrutinized a glass vial which held tear gas, and didn't figure that out, either.

"Newfangled burglar tools," he decided.

Thelma got in the front seat. Zeke slid behind the wheel and drove, but not toward the police station.

"Hey," Rush said. "You're going in the wrong direction."

"You crazy?"

"Eh?"

"You didn't think," Zeke said in an amazed voice, "that I would do anything except kill you." Then Zeke suddenly seized the girl Thelma, and used the spare handcuff to fasten her to Rush and the others. "You too, Thelma," Zeke said.

RUSH WRITHED, not having expected any such words from an eccentric old fellow who, according to what he had just been reading in the newspapers, was Tulsa's leading philanthropist. He had a great deal that he wanted to say, but before he could get it out, one of the ox-shaped men jerked the handcuff which linked them together and growled, "Oh, don't argue with the old frog. He means it, all right. He's taking us out in the oil fields somewhere, and will probably poison us the way he poisoned Harold Schraft."

"How was that?" Rush asked quickly.

"How was Harold poisoned? The old frog used the same trick he employed thirty years ago. He's got some kind of poison. Picked it up in Sicily one time when he had to lam out of the country for a while. I don't know what it is. But it sure works. He smears it on the frog, and you think the frog is just slimy or something. It don't kill the frog for a while. But you handle the frog, and you die."

"The L.E.M.A. meddler picked up the mashed frog in the post office and put it in a bottle. So he died, too. That it?"

"That's it."

Zeke slowed the car and turned his head. He spoke to Rush. "You know what you've done? You've asked questions, and got answers, so now I couldn't let you go if I wanted to."

"If I've got you figured out right," Rush said, "you didn't want to very bad."

"Nope," Zeke admitted. "I didn't."

"He's a mean old devil," said one of the blocky men. "He always was. Paw always said he wished he'd drowned Zeke the mornin' after he was born."

"You are brothers?"

"We ain't proud of it."

"Zeke used to be leader of the gang," the other thick-bodied man explained. "We called him the Old Frog, on account of that frog trick he used on people he didn't like."

"Shut up!" Zeke snarled.

"Oh, shut up yourself! You're a hell of a brother, you are! You hit it lucky in oil, and disowned the rest of us. You didn't even cough up for a lawyer when Harold got caught robbing a bank."

Rush glanced at the girl. "Are you really a member of the family?"

The girl tried to speak, couldn't, and shook her head.

Zeke said, "She's just a little girl who was getting suspicious. Weren't you, Thelma?"

"Yes," said Thelma. "You were acting very strange lately."

THE CAR followed the Broken Arrow road for a short distance, then turned south again. It came to a bridge and crossed and passed through a small dark town. After that, it swung off the main road, where the going was bumpy. Oil derricks began appearing in the moonlight, more and more of them. It was distressingly silent in the car.

"Oliver," Rush said, "why don't you think of a gag?"

Oliver swallowed, and mumbled, "Maybe I won't be a radio gag man after all."

"You remember that book the detective wrote, the one I was telling you about?" Rush asked.

"The one by a detective named Ricky Rivers?"

"That's it. In his book, Ricky Rivers said not to mind getting scared. He said that it is the nature of any normal man to get scared, and if you don't, you had better not be a detective. Not only that, you had better go to a hospital where they examine minds, because you're not normal."

"I'm scared," Oliver confessed.

"So am I," Rush assured him. "So we are both normal. I will be a great detective, you will be a great radio gag man, according to Ricky Rivers."

Zeke asked sourly, "What the blazes kind of talk is that? You sound like two nuts."

Rush grumbled, "We're just trying to bolster up our courage."

The car jumped over rough ground and brush switched noisily at the chassis. A shack, a typical oil field shack of plain boards, loomed alongside, and the car stopped.

"Out and march," Zeke said.

The shack's interior was dusty. There was a table made of boards, some boxes, one kitchen chair and a gas stove which was remarkably rusted. Gas piped into the shack was not remarkable; gas was used everywhere here in the oil fields. Zeke glanced about, and was satisfied.

"Here's how it will go," he said. "You got away from me, see, and you drove off. Last I saw of you. You came here to hide out, and you lit that old gas stove, only it didn't work right, and the gas got you. All I've got to do is turn the gas on, and take the handcuffs off you later. I'll leave them on Thelma. That will make it look better."

Rush said, "What still puzzles me is the reason."

"Simple," Zeke said. "These brothers of mine got together and decided they didn't like the idea of the giving my money to charity. Seemed to think *they* were my heirs. They came to me and said they were going to prove I was an ex-outlaw, and put me in jail, if I didn't pay them off. I had to stop that."

"So he set out to kill us," one of the square men added. "He sent Harold a frog."

"We're sorry about you, kinda," the other blocky man told Rush. "You see, we knew you had a reputation, so we figured we would sort of grab you and throw you in Zeke's backyard, and let you work out the situation."

Rush nodded. He had already decided that was what had happened.

"Zeke doesn't seem like the kind of a man who would give all that money away," he said thoughtfully.

"Zeke is a show-off," one of the brothers advised. "He always was a show-off. And a little bit goofy."

"But smart," Zeke said proudly. "Smart as they come. That's me."

It was plain that he knew the layout of the shack thoroughly, because he went to a plank cupboard in the corner and dragged out a long rope, a cowboy lariat, which he uncoiled and tossed over one of the two-by-four braces that extended across over their heads, below the rafters, after which it became plain that he was going to anchor them, all linked with handcuffs, so that they could not escape while the gas was flowing into the shack and asphyxiating them.

RUSH LOOKED down at his feet and said, "Darn it, this thing is coming loose," and began to use his left toe to pry at his right heel. The heel seemed to be loose.

"No, you don't!" Zeke yelled, and leaped forward. Zeke threw himself against Rush, unbalancing him, forcing him to stop tampering with the shoe. "I'm suspicious of you!" Zeke snarled. "You probably got some trick in that shoe heel."

He got down on all fours and grabbed Rush's shoe and examined the heel closely, then became puzzled and finally tore the heel completely off the shoe, grunting with the effort. It was merely an ordinary rubber heel.

"Say," Zeke growled, bewildered. "What in trumpet—"

Rush had set himself by that time, and he fell forward suddenly upon Zeke. He struck, not with his fists, but with the inside of his left elbow. The blow landed. Zeke barked "Ouch!" and retreated, then menaced Rush with the ornate inlaid pistol. "What was the idea of that funny business?"

Rush showed his teeth in what he tried to make a pleased grin. He didn't feel very cheerful, however, because he wasn't sure his gadget had functioned.

The gadget was a hypodermic needle, containing a strong stupefying drug, and concealed inside a rubber hide-out which was cemented to the inside of his elbow—where anyone feeling over his arm in a search would, if they encountered the hard protuberance, think they had touched one of the hard bones in the elbow.

Zeke felt of his shoulder, where the blow had landed. He unbuttoned his shirt and put his hand inside to explore.

"Say, did you stick me with something?" he growled.

Rush said nothing. Zeke scowled, pulled out a match, struck it, and turned gas into the rusted stove. There was a *swoosh!* of a noise and flame rushed across the burners.

"The gas comes through all right," he mumbled. "Now I'll turn it out—"

He stopped and blinked his eyes, then felt of his face. "Damn it! I feel dizzy." And he staggered when he straightened.

Zeke dropped his gun, swore thickly, and doubled Over to fumble for it.

The two blocky men lunged forward.

"Wait!" Rush shouted. "He'll be out in a minute. One of you will get shot!"

They paid no attention. They fell upon their brother, dragging Rush, the girl and Oliver along. All of them together made a confused pile on the floor.

Zeke still had strength. He got hold of his gun, and twisted around. One of the thick men struggled with him, and when he could not get the gun out of Zeke's hands, forced the muzzle back so that it pointed at Zeke's head.

When the gun exploded, the bullet went in somewhere and came out through the top of Zeke's head.

Rush kicked too late, and sent the gun flying out through the door.

After that, they yanked each other around in a furious brawl, handcuff links grinding. Because of the manacles, the fighting was done mostly with their feet. Probably three minutes passed before Rush and Oliver managed to kick the two ox-shaped men into limpness.

Rush puffed, "The cuff keys—in Zeke's pocket!"

THE POLICE were a little bitter about it. Concerning the two chunky men, they were not displeased, particularly after they checked over their fingerprints and found that they were wanted for an armored-truck robbery in Chicago, a murder in Memphis and a bank job in Dallas.

"But you sure played heck with Tulsa's leading philanthropist," complained the desk sergeant.

"I didn't kill him," Rush said.

"Well, maybe no, technically."

"Anyway," Rush explained, "his lawyers were down looking at the remains. They say he had already fixed it up to give all his money to charity, and the papers had been signed, so the arrangements will stick."

"Oh, say!" the desk sergeant exclaimed. He fumbled around in the rubble on his desk and came up with an envelope. "This arrived in the morning mail, addressed to you."

As Rush expected, the envelope contained nothing whatever but the other half of the ten-thousand-dollar bill. It was from the mysterious person who spoke as the voice of Bufa, the toad, of course. Rush glared and thought of violent words and began saying them out loud.

"Here! Here! Such language!" the cop said.

"You should have heard me when the first half of the bill came," Rush said, and went out and found Oliver, who was looking thoughtfully at Thelma.

It had become daylight, and Thelma in the light of day was decidedly worth a thoughtful examination.

"I have figured out another one," Oliver said. "It goes: Pat—I have a complete education. Mike—'No, you haven't. You're a bachelor.'" Oliver chuckled. "Not bad, eh? I may make a radio gag man after all."

Rush took Oliver's arm.

"Oliver," Rush said, "we haven't been doing a very good job fooling each other."

"Eh?"

"You know that book—the one by Ricky Rivers, the detective? Have you any idea why I mentioned it?"

"Well—"

"The truth is, I recognized you, Oliver," he said. "You are Ricky Rivers yourself."

Oliver sighed. "I was afraid you had guessed. Yes, I am really Ricky Rivers. I am here in Tulsa watching a loan-company president who skipped. He is staying at that hotel, and I am supposed to find the money he took when he skipped. Personally, I think he has already spent it."

"Why did you try to fool me, Oliver?"

"I wanted to see you use those gadgets to solve a crime. I had read about them."

"That's what I figured," Rush said. "So I fooled you. I thought I would not use a single gadget at any time, only it got so tough I had to."

"That is why you didn't use any gadgets this time?"

"Yes."

Oliver sighed. "What do you say we join Thelma and cooperate in consoling her."

"Consoling Thelma," Rush admitted, "should be very much worth the effort."

THE FRIGHTENED YACHTSMEN

MURDER TURNS A PLEASURE
YACHT INTO A HELL-SHIP!

CHAPTER I

ALL WERE SCARED

IN THE TROPICAL sky there was nowhere a trace of a
cloud, and the sun sent down glittering white heat that
made the eyes ache.

Under this sun, the Caribbean sea was as slick as oiled
glass and as blue as a rifle barrel.

The rowboat was adrift on the sea. It was a rowboat that
was about ten feet long and made of a light framework
covered with canvas, varnished inside and painted white
outside. There was only one oar in the boat, and no food,
no water. There was, however, a steel box a little larger than
a suitcase, equipped with a handle.

The man stood in the rowboat and waved the oar. The
man's skin was sunburned and blistered, his eyes blood-
shot. He wore a brown undershirt and brown trousers and
brown canvas sneakers, all in bad condition, and while he
was not a large man, there were some amazing muscles in
his bare shoulders and arms, more muscles than men ordinarily have. He had tied his ragged brown shirt to the end
of the oar as a flag.

Those on the yacht saw, and the craft turned toward the
man adrift in the boat. It was a glittering yacht of white and
mahogany and brass, possibly seventy feet long; it needed
painting and the Diesel engines were worn and pounding,

but the defects were not apparent until the craft drew close to the man in the rowboat.

The man sank down in the rowboat, his strength apparently having fled. He gestured a feeble and glad welcome with both hands. When they came alongside and put a rope ladder over, he made three unsuccessful efforts to climb—stubbornly insisting on carrying his steel box. From the yacht deck they called, "Leave the box! We'll get it!" But he paid no attention. So finally two sailors got down in the boat and helped the man—he kept a tight clutch on the box all the time—to the yacht deck.

"Water!" the rescued man croaked at once.

Everyone on board the yacht had gathered around to stare. There were nine of them—eight men and a girl.

All nine persons on the yacht were scared.

They were frightened, and the existence of their terror had nothing to do with the man they had just rescued—the terror had been there before he came. None of the staring people on the yacht threw up their hands in horror, nor did they send furtive glances about; it was simply that there was definite tension in their manner that showed that something was wrong.

"Dammit, give me some water!" the rescued man yelled wildly. He sounded as if he was cackling.

One of the scared yachtsmen, a wide and red-faced man, spoke. "My nose was itching all morning," he complained.

"What's that mean, MacCoggan?" The one girl spoke with a pleasant voice. She was a long girl with a nice smile—even if it wasn't a natural smile.

"Oh, you know that one, Sara," MacCoggan told her. "Meant we were going to have company."

MacCOGGAN WAS a strong man. He picked up the fellow they had rescued, the latter still clinging to the steel case, and carried him below. MacCoggan was not even breathing rapidly when he placed his burden on a bunk, indicating he was not as soft as he looked.

The cabin was typical boat accommodation—a tall man standing with outstretched arms could have spanned any of its dimensions.

The rescued man drank some water.

"I was sailing from Bimini to Gun Cay in a thirty-foot sloop and the boat snagged a floating log or something," he explained. "The centerboard hit hardest, and ripped part of the centerboard trunk open, and the water came in. You've no idea how damned fast a boat can sink."

"How long ago was that?" MacCoggan asked.

"Two days."

"You're lucky."

"I know. I could have got shipwrecked during some bad weather. Been the end of me."

MacCoggan took a pinch of something out of his coat pocket and threw it over his left shoulder.

"Why did you do that?"

MacCoggan grinned. "Luck. It's salt."

"Oh."

None of the rescuers asked any more questions, and the rescued man did not speak, so there was silence for a while. Then a man grunted and stepped to the steel chest.

He was a thin brown man, sunburned until his skin was almost as dark as that of a blacksnake. He began fumbling with the chest that the rescued man had carried so carefully.

The owner reared up on the bunk. "Get away from that!" he yelled.

The thin brown man looked surprised. He said, "What's eatin' this ickie? I'm only gonna gander at what he has in his dog house, and he rides in with a squawk like a gob stick."

The girl said, "After all, Rory, the box is his own private property."

Rory said, "Humph!" and wheeled around and walked out, leaving silence behind.

The rescued man asked, "Just what kind of language was that fellow speaking?"

"Rory? He's a cat."

"Eh?"

"A musician."

MacCoggan snorted. "You overrate him, Sara. Rory is plenty corny. He's just been lucky."

The musical status of Rory did not seem important to the girl. She soon walked out of the cabin, then the others also departed, all but MacCoggan, who stood staring down thoughtfully at the rescued man. There was nothing but MacCoggan and the rescued man and stillness in the cabin.

"Anything I can get you?" MacCoggan asked. "Little drinkie, maybe?"

"No drinkie." The rescued man breathed heavily, as if from exhaustion. "But you might tell me something."

"Be glad to."

"I think I heard"—the man's voice sounded weak and his fingers twitched—"someone mention a name. Nick. I know a yachtsman named Nick. He might be the same Nick. Mind finding out? Or did I imagine it?"

MacCoggan grinned. "I'm Nick."

"Eh?"

"Nick—Nick Davis MacCoggan. Sometimes I just use the Nick Davis part. Back when I was doing four a day, I used it all the time."

"Four a day?"

"Vaudeville. But I produce Broadway musicals now."

The rescued man suddenly shed all trace of physical exhaustion. He sprang out of the bunk with agility, skipped to the door, jerked it closed and shot the bolt.

"You must be the man who sent me the radio message to get on this boat," he said. "Yesterday, that was. Remember?" MacCOGGAN SCRATCHED his head, above his left ear, then took out a cigarette and put fire to it. "You are—"

"Clickell Rush," the rescued man explained. "The Gadget Man, if you want to give me the name the blasted newspapers use."

"You're a detective?"

"Yes."

"You picked a hell of a strange way of getting on board."

"Didn't your radio message yesterday say to keep anybody from knowing I was a detective?"

"But who would have thought—I'll be damned—how'd you manage?"

Rush said, "You remember that your radiogram gave the exact location and course of the boat. Well, that told me where I could meet the boat. Flew down from New York, then hired a seaplane to drop me and the rowboat in the path of the yacht. Plane was to come back this afternoon late, to pick me up in case you missed, or sooner, if the weather turned bad."

MacCoggan looked around until he found a wooden chair, which he tapped with his knuckles, then handed the chair to Rush and advised, "Knock wood. It keeps your luck good." Rush knocked wood, then with his toe nudged the steel box which was lying at his feet.

"My luck is in there," he said, meaning the box.

"I don't understand," MacCoggan said. Then he decided he did know. "Gadgets. I get it," he said. "I've read about you. They gave you that nickname of Gadget Man because you invented a few thousand gadgets for catching criminals and tried to sell the gadgets to police departments. You turned detective yourself to demonstrate that the gadgets were workable."

"Something like that."

MacCoggan pointed at the case. "You've got your gadgets in there?"

"Yes."

MacCoggan looked at the box, then he stared at Click Rush, and after a while chuckling began to shake his stomach; then he said, "This is rich! It's as cockeyed as a stew-bum's dream, but you've got everybody thinking you're a rescued castaway." He went on chuckling.

Rush said, "Let's get down to business."

MacCoggan stopped chuckling. "What do you want to know?"

*BY PULLING A SILK THREAD, RUSH COULD MAKE THE STUFFED
SPARROW ON THE PERISCOPE FLAP ITS WINGS...*

"Was I right in counting nine persons on the boat, excepting myself?"

"Right."

"Where is the yacht headed?"

"Blowfish Cay. It's an island on the edge of the Bahama Bank."

"And the object of the trip?"

"There you've got me," MacCoggan said instantly. "Personally, I'm just a guest. Sara owns the boat, and I've known her for a long time, because her foster father and I were good friends for years before he died."

Rush asked, "Then you don't know what this trouble is about?"

"No," said MacCoggan sincerely. "I don't."

"When were you attacked?"

"You mean—oh, that. That was two days ago. I told you a lot over the radio, didn't I?"

"Any idea who did it?"

"No—none. I was just standing by the rail and someone rushed me with a chair and knocked me overboard. I yelled, and the yacht turned around and picked me up. I didn't see who it was."

"What are the others scared of?"

"Well, we all figure someone has gone insane aboard. We don't know which one of us it is. Naturally everybody is worried."

"I'll bet."

MacCoggan sighed deeply and said, "I shouldn't have come. The day before we sailed, I accidentally opened an umbrella in the house, watched a train out of sight, changed my sock after I had put it wrong side out, and killed a spider. All of those things mean bad luck."

"Not superstitious?"

MacCoggan looked indignant. "To contradict the possible existence of guiding omens is to deny that there is an extrasensory influence on our lives—such as luck, for example. You know very well there is good luck and bad luck. Therefore—"

Rush said, "Speaking of luck—it's lucky you knew Jake Smith."

"Huh?"

"Jake Smith. The man who suggested that you radio me for help."

"Oh, yes." MacCoggan grinned. "To be sure. Jake Smith, my old friend."

Rush took a deep breath.

"You tell a nice lie."

"Huh?"

RUSH GOT between MacCoggan and the door and continued, "I must be slipping. Or maybe the sun was hotter than it seemed in the rowboat and softened my head. I should have thought of Jake Smith first thing, shouldn't I?"

"Have you suddenly gone crazy?" MacCoggan asked incredulously.

Rush sat on the edge of the bunk, crossed one leg over the other and began absent-minded explorations in a hole in the leg of his brown trousers, using two fingers of his right hand for the probing.

"There isn't any Jake Smith."

"There… there *isn't?*" MacCoggan swallowed.

"He was what you might call a figment of my imagination—which makes you out a liar."

With the two fingers that had been exploring in the hole in his trousers, Rush fished out a device which in many respects resembled a metal automatic pencil, the contrivance having been concealed in a sheath which was strapped to his leg with adhesive tape, where it was conveniently accessible. When he pressed the lever on the side of this gadget, a thin stream of liquid squirted out of the point with great force.

However, a moment before the liquid came out of the device, Rush pointed at the metal case on the floor by saying loudly, "Why don't you open that box? You'll find something interesting," he said, distracting MacCoggan's attention to the box, so that MacCoggan did not at first become aware of the thin spray of liquid falling over his chest and face. Then he lifted a hand, dabbed at his face.

"What the—"

Rush slid the pencil-shaped device back into its concealed sheath, so that by the time it occurred to MacCoggan to look at him, he was feeling of his left cheek and looking innocent.

"Felt something wet on my face," MacCoggan muttered.

"Yes," Rush agreed. "Spray must have flew through the porthole. I'll close it."

He got up and went to the porthole—careful all the while not to draw air into his lungs—and instead of closing the port, thrust his head outside and breathed pure air while he waited for the gas to overcome MacCoggan.

MacCoggan said, "Hell, this don't smell like sea water," in a rather thick voice, then mumbled something else that was not intelligible, after which he said clearly, "I feel faint." Then a chair grunted as he sat in it heavily.

Rush held his breath, opened the door, then returned and stood with his head out of the porthole. He had gotten a little of the gas himself, enough to make him slightly dizzy. He stood there for some time.

When he turned, MacCoggan sat slumped in the chair, stupefied rather than unconscious. Rush began going through his pockets. MacCoggan made feeble efforts to resist, but they were ineffectual.

The only thing of importance which MacCoggan's pockets held was a sheaf of business cards indicating his name was Joseph MacCoggan.

Not Nick Davis MacCoggan.

CHAPTER 11

DEATH HIRED A DETECTIVE

WHEN RUSH OPENED the cabin door and stepped outside, the girl, Sara, was standing there. She wore slacks, and she was tall enough to wear them well.

"Did you hurt him?" she asked.

"Huh?" Rush swallowed. "Hurt who?"

She took his arm, said, "Come on," in a low voice and led him into the adjoining cabin. She pointed to an electrical amplifier and headset. A modern listening-in device. Obviously, it was hooked to a microphone concealed in the cabin where Rush had been—MacCoggan's cabin.

"I heard everything you two said," the girl explained. "Did you hurt him?"

"He'll be all right in half an hour, probably."

On the bunk against the outer wall of the cabin was a second dictagraph, exactly like the first one. This one was hooked up to wires that led to a microphone somewhere else on the yacht.

Rush pointed at the second listening-in device. "Where does *that* one go?

"To Rory's cabin."

"Rory—he is the swing-music lad. The cat?"

"Yes. Haven't you ever heard his orchestra on the air? Doctor Rory's Melody Medicine."

"Nope."

"He's really quite good."

"So good that you had to spot a dictagraph in his room?" Rush asked dryly.

The girl hesitated. "I was speaking of his music."

Rush looked at the girl, and she was easy to look at—so much so that his thoughts kept jumping over where they had no business to be, tending to make him more confused and completely mystified.

He said, "If this keeps up, everyone aboard is going to know I'm a detective. I would hate that. I thought that business of being a shipwrecked sailor adrift in a boat was a very good shenanigan."

"It was slick," the girl said.

"Yes, but friend MacCoggan was more clever. And so were you."

"I was trying to find out things," the girl explained.

"So am I." Rush considered. "The next thing I would like to find out is about Nick."

"Nick? What about Nick?"

"Who is he?"

Instead of answering, the girl left the cabin and entered the one adjoining, where she stood staring at MacCoggan for some time. She went over to MacCoggan and touched him and his eyes followed her, although he did not move any other part of his body. The girl returned to her own cabin. Rush followed her and closed the door, then said, "It's only a strong anaesthetic in gas form, so don't worry."

The girl nodded.

"Ever hear of Martin Dameron?" she asked unexpectedly.

RUSH DID not reply, an answer hardly seeming necessary. If anyone in the world had not heard of Martin Dameron, they had never heard music. Martin Dameron was a composer, and, more than that, unquestionably the most famous composer of this generation, probably of the century. The music of Martin Dameron had been played so much that the general public had taken it for granted that he was one of the old classical masters. There had probably been some general astonishment When the newspapers had headlined the fact of his death—six months ago. Millions of people had taken it for granted that he was an old master. Martin Dameron had been legendary long before his death, his musical scores possessing an immortal something which made them a joy now, and a joy forever. They were ageless, those compositions. But Martin Dameron himself had died only six months ago.

"What has Martin Dameron got to do with Nick?" Rush asked.

"Nick was his secretary," the girl explained. "A long time ago, Nick was a composer himself. But he lost his touch. Nick had a great deal of technical knowledge of music, but no ability whatever to create. Martin Dameron had a fabulous creative facility, but knew almost nothing about music. I think Nick was always a little contemptuous of Dameron's lack of musical knowledge. As I said, Nick was Martin Dameron's secretary, until Martin died, six months ago."

"And you?"

"I… I was Martin Dameron's ward."

The term "ward" which wealthy and famous men sometimes applied to pretty young women constantly in their association could cover an assortment of meanings. Rush thought of some of the meanings, and must have smiled.

The girl said angrily, "My grandmother, I imagine, would have slapped your face for that smirk."

"In which case," Rush said, "I would have slapped back. However, I'm really sorry. I apologize."

The girl said. "When I was seven years old, Martin Dameron's car crashed in to another machine in which my father and mother were riding, and they were killed. It was no one's fault, but Martin Dameron took me and brought me up. I had not seen him in two years before he died. I was in France, in school. After his death, I learned I was Martin Dameron's legal heir—had there been anything to inherit."

Rush nodded, remembering. "Martin Dameron died almost penniless, didn't he?"

"Martin Dameron was a remarkable man," Sara said. "He managed to spend every cent of an income of two hundred and fifty thousand dollars a year."

"If I ever make two hundred and fifty thousand a year, hope I can spend it," Rush said. "That would be what I call a successful job of living."

The yacht plowed ahead, hardly rolling at all, the bows throwing water aside with a sound as if a giant was washing his hands continuously. The motors were old, and clankings and poundings came monotonously from the engine room.

"In case I didn't tell you," Rush added, "I'm completely puzzled by all this. A man named Nick hired me by radio, saying he had been attacked two days ago, and wanted protection. That's all the information I have."

"When did you say Nick hired you?"

"Yesterday."

"Strange," the girl said. "Nick died day before yesterday."

"But he hired me yesterday!" Rush exploded.

"I doubt it—Nick was lying dead in his cabin all day yesterday!"

IT WAS a small cabin in the stern and not a desirable one because it was directly over the propellers where there was noise and vibration when the boat was under way. There were flowers in the little cabin, all of the flowers that had been on the yacht, probably. They were wilted now.

Nick was a triangular man. His legs and hips were small, making the taper of the triangle, and his shoulders were wide, forming the base. There was almost no neck between his head and his shoulders. He had been no beauty.

Also, he had evidently been beaten badly before he died.

Rush hastily replaced the sheet. They backed out of the cabin. Rush had never been able to accustom himself to death—if anything, his squeamish sensations became worse each time. He dug a brown handkerchief out of his pocket and blotted his face.

"What did he die of?"

"We don't know," the girl said. "Rory's a doctor, and he examined—"

"Wait a minute," Rush said. "I thought the doctor part of Rory's name was a phony."

"He's really a licensed physician," Sara explained. "He examined poor Nick. He decided it was some kind of epileptic fit—as a result of the beating."

"Who beat him?"

"We don't know."

"Do you know why?"

"No."

Rush said with growing impatience, "Why not tell me what is wrong aboard this hooker? Why did someone summon me here, using Nick's name?"

The girl compressed her lips and said, "There is nothing wrong on this boat that I know of."

Rush put his handkerchief away. "Nobody is worried about anything?"

"Everything is all right."

"Then why were you eavesdropping with a dictagraph?"

The girl turned away. Rush took her wrist. She jerked free.

"Everything I've told you is truth!" she snapped. "But I'm not going to tell you anything more!"

Putting on his most pleasant, smiling, worthy-of-your-confidence expression, Rush asked, "Why not?"

"Because you're a tremendous liar."

"A liar! *Me?*"

"Yes."

"Name one lie," Rush requested indignantly.

"You say someone called you by radio from this boat?"

"Yes."

"There isn't any radio on this yacht!" the girl said, and wheeled and walked off.

CHAPTER III

BLOWFISH CAY

R **USH WENT TO** look.

There was no radio on the yacht.

Rush went back to the cabin where MacCoggan was still sprawled in the chair. MacCoggan had recovered enough to glower and struggle and upset his chair, after which he squirmed on the floor. Rush stretched on the bunk, grimacing—there was nothing particularly comfortable about the artificial sunburn which he had put on his back with chemicals—and did some thinking.

It appeared that no one could possibly have summoned him to this yacht.

He had, however, been summoned.

The messenger boy had delivered a radiogram to his apartment in New York, and after reading it, Rush had written out a telegram in reply, which the boy had taken away. The reply had requested the exact course of the yacht. A few hours later, the same messenger boy had brought an answer, giving the location of the yacht, and its course. Rush had written out a message stating that he would take the job investigating the attempt on the life of the unknown Nick, the consideration for the services being one thousand dollars in cash, and expenses.

There was just one peculiarity about the matter of the radiograms.

The messenger had seemed a little old for the job.

Rush rubbed his jaw and did some reflecting on his own past, which might help explain what had happened. If so, it might go back to the time when he had imagined himself an inventor, when he had perfected hundreds of scientific gadgets for catching criminals, and had tried to sell the gadgets to the New York police. He must have been gullible, he supposed now. He had supposed the inventions were sensible, because they worked; but nobody else seemed to think so. The newspapers had printed some very humorous—to their readers, but not to Rush—stuff about it.

Then Bufa had gotten hold of Rush.

It was Rush's conviction that Bufa was some kind of a nut. All Rush knew about Bufa, really, was that Bufa had a voice. Rush had found a remarkably ugly toad in his room, and inside the toad was a wired-wireless "transceiver" by which it was possible to communicate over the city electric-light wires with another similar device located somewhere—and no way of telling where, either—in the city. Bufa, the voice of this toad, it seemed, wanted Rush to solve unusual crimes employing his scientific gadgets, and get ten thousand dollars as payment for each crime. It had seemed wonderful, too good to be true. Rush was about broke.

But it hadn't stopped with solving one unusual crime. The thing had gone on and on; and when Rush got tired of risking his neck and tried to put a stop to it, Bufa began framing him into uncomfortable predicaments where he had to work, whether he wished or not.

Another trouble about quitting was that lately Rush had tried promoting the manufacture of some of his supposedly more sensible inventions, and was losing his shirt at it. He needed money.

When this harmless-looking job of finding out why a man named Nick had been attacked on a yacht in the Caribbean—when that opportunity had presented—it had seemed a nice way of making a dollar—or a thousand of them.

Now the thing seemed to have acquired some suspicious ramifications. Not the least of these being the apparent impossibility of anyone having hired Rush from this boat.

Rush frowned at MacCoggan. "Ever hear of Bufa?"

"Eh?" MacCoggan scowled while he considered. "No. Why?"

"It just occurred to me," Rush said thoughtfully, "that maybe Bufa engineered me into this. Maybe Bufa rigged those radiograms that got me down here." Then he thought of something else and sprang out of the bunk, howled, "Hell's bells! In that case I'm working for *one* thousand dollars instead of the usual ten thousand!"

MacCoggan had recovered enough to get up and sit on the chair again.

Someone on deck yelled, "There's Blowfish Cay!"

BLOWFISH CAY might have been a white rag lying on the indigo table of the sea—a white rag with a bit of green lace along the high edge. The white was coral sand and waves creaming on the beach; the green was tropical vegetation, palms and mangroves and cactus and lignum vitae and palmetto.

While Rush leaned on the rail, a man came up behind him and said, "You seem to be feeling more like."

Rush turned. It was Rory. "I've been getting a rejuvenating treatment," Rush explained. He added, "Didn't recognize you when you spoke English."

The yacht, went charging in, dragging a squirming white wake, like a long ostrich plume in a breeze, along behind. There was a flat beach, bared to the tropical sea. A few gulls circled above, two fat pelicans swam toward the boat, unafraid because they didn't know man. Some Portuguese man O' war, like inflated toy balloons, purple, floated on the water. And the water wasn't blue now. Shallowness had turned it amber, and in the crystal clear depths sea fans waved and coral was a grotesque maze in which a rainbow galaxy of tropical fish swim.

The anchor went down, chain sounding like an angry lion.

Rush asked, "What's here?"

"Ever hear a long-hair named Martin Dameron?" Rory asked.

Rush scratched his head and faked being puzzled and finally muttered, "Seems like I've heard the name. Wasn't he a movie actor?"

"You must be a corny ick," Rory said disgustedly. "Martin Dameron was the hottest one that ever did a joint or wrote a legit."

"Sometime you can translate for me," Rush said. "In the meantime—what has Martin Dameron got to do with this island?"

"Martin Dameron lived on Blowfish Cay until he died six months ago.

"He died here?"

"Yes."

"Now, can you tell me why everybody on this boat is scared stiff?"

Rory looked at Rush, something black and ugly on his face. "Take a tip, ickie," he said grimly, "and keep your nose clean."

He walked away and joined four sailors forward. They began taking the cover off one of the tenders, preparing to go ashore. The girl, Sara, came out, wearing a sun hat as large as a cowboy's sombrero. MacCoggan appeared and leaned against the rail, looking a little ill. Then he moved away.

Rush counted them mentally, and got nine. All of them Were on deck. All tense. All trying not to turn their backs to the others any more than they had to.

It came to Rush suddenly that the sailors, too, were mixed up in this thing, whatever it was. All of them were in it. And he, Rush, didn't have the slightest idea what it was all about. He felt irritated. Angered.

Rush raised his voice.

"Wait a minute!" Rush shouted.

They stared at him. The two pelicans, frightened by his loud voice, batted at their wings against the water, and took off.

"I'm a detective," Rush bellowed. "I was hired to come down here and take care of this mess."

He added a couple of lies for good measure.

"I know the truth about what happened to Nick," he yelled. "And I'm going to settle it right now, before anybody goes on that island. I've got all the truth on this."

He had no plan, and no purpose except feeding his rage some satisfaction. They were staring at him. He glowered back. He had two teargas grenades, one in each hip pocket, and in one of his other trouser pockets was a transparent hood of tough cellophane-like material, elastic at the bottom, which he could pull over his head to serve as a temporary mask.

He was just about to reach for his tear gas when someone tried to shoot the girl.

CHAPTER IV
A PROBLEM ON AN ISLAND

THE GUN MUZZLE had edged out of a porthole, and the girl must have been lucky and seen it, because she was springing wildly backward when the weapon made a loud noise. The bullet missed her. She dived behind a corner of the deckhouse.

One of the sailors who had been helping prepare the tender for the water suddenly leaped for the girl. He seized her and tried to hurl her back in range of the killer at the porthole.

Rush—he was dumfounded, for he had thought he had counted the whole party of nine on deck—charged the girl's assailant. He did not use pleasant tactics. He jumped, hit feet first on the fellow's back.

The man made a noise like an old-time automobile horn, then fell. Rush seized the girl, skidded her through a companionway. He followed. They bounced down steps and became a pile at the bottom.

"Who tried to shoot you?" Rush barked.

"I don't know."

The man who had seized the girl was trying to get to his feet. A fire extinguisher hung on the bulkhead. Rush got it, aimed with care, and bounced it off the man's head.

One of the group on deck began shooting with a high-powered rifle. The bullets ripped through deck and bulkheads, flooring and bottom planking.

Rush said, "Why, blast 'em! They'll sink the boat!"

The man with the high-powered rifle must have heard his voice. Bullets clubbed out splinters very close. Rush got the girl's wrist, dragged her forward.

"How did you find out the truth?" she asked.

"Didn't," Rush said.

A fist fight started on deck. There was some cursing, but mostly blows. Finally one of the participants screamed, "Bring that rifle, Rory!" Rush didn't recognize the voice, so it must have been one of the sailors.

A moment later, MacCoggan fell down into the cabin with a sailor hanging to him. They pounded each other. Rush picked up a long brass chart case and walloped the handiest combatant, which happened to be the sailor. The sailor jumped back, scrambled up the companion and escaped, although Rush threw the chart case at him.

MacCoggan wallowed on the floor.

"Thanks," he gulped.

Rush leaned over and swung a fist. MacCoggan became senseless.

"Don't know who my friends are yet," Rush told the wide-eyed Sara.

There was a whining and grinding noise forward. Rush had once purchased a boat in hopes of living aboard it, and escaping the unwelcome attentions of Bufa, the mysterious voice of the toad, which kept causing him to get involved in unusual crimes, so he knew the kind of a noise an electric winch makes in bringing up an anchor.

"Seems as if they changed their minds about anchoring," Rush said.

He found a hatch, pulled his transparent hood over his head, then tossed out his tear-gas bombs. They sounded like big firecrackers. Soon men began swearing and falling over things. Rush closed the hatch.

The girl snapped, "But you said on deck that you knew all the truth."

"That was an experiment," Rush explained, lifting his transparent hood for the words.

"It might be suicide, too."

The starters clattered, the engines thumped and pounded, and the yacht picked up speed for a while. Then it stopped with a loud thump and an upward lunge, as if it had tried to jump over something and half succeeded. **RUSH SHOVED** himself away from the bulkhead against which he had been piled and explained, rather needlessly, "They must have beached her."

He listened and decided everyone on deck was leaping ashore in order to escape the tear gas.

The girl's eyes were watering, so instead of lifting his hood and speaking to her, he clutched her arm and hauled her to the cabin, where he had left his metal case. He had exhausted the air in his hood and was feeling dizzy, so he closed the door, made a roll out of a blanket and slung it at the bottom of the door, then closed the porthole. He lifted the lower edge of the hood to his upper lip, so that his mouth was exposed for breathing. The gas stung his lungs, but his eyes remained usable.

"I wonder who tried to shoot you," he said.

The girl began, "I told you I didn't—"

"—you didn't know. Yes, so you said. But could there have been a stowaway aboard?"

"I doubt it. I searched the boat three times for stowaways. I imagine each one of the others searched at least once."

"Why all the searching?"

At this point, the high-powered rifle went to work again. Now and then, a slug would hit something thick enough to stop it.

Rush muttered, "He keeps that up, and he's going to hit somebody," and opened his equipment box and took out his compressed-air grenade thrower. The device bore general resemblance to an air rifle, although the barrel was shot-gun sized; air could be jacked into the thing with a lever, and a tiny gauge showed the pressure and the approximate distance which a grenade would be thrown when the gun was held at a forty-five-degree angle. The grenades were bullet-shaped, would drop into the barrel, and the confines of the barrel would hold down the tiny firing levers until after discharge. Rush, when perfecting the device, had visualized the thing having military value for trench warfare, but the army had not been particularly enthusiastic.

The girl came over, held her smarting eyes open with her fingers, and looked into the box.

"What an amazing litter of things!" she said.

"I don't see," Rush said peevishly, "why people insist on referring to the things I invent as litter."

He put a smoke-cartridge in the compressed air device, calculated wind direction through the porthole, and dropped the missile in the nearby thicket of palmetto. It exploded into a thing the size of a black bear, and grew. Rush launched four more of the cartridges, and the breeze carried their combined black pall over the yacht.

He fired some tear gas for good measure. The rifle stopped banging on shore.

"You stay here," Rush told the girl.

He went out, found MacCoggan, grasped the man's arms and dragged him back into the cabin where the gadget chest stood. MacCoggan was still semiconscious, although his eyes were watering and his chest kept bouncing up and down from his effort to cough out the irritating tear gas.

The girl seemed disgusted with Rush.

"If I had *one* friend on the boat," she said, "it was MacCoggan.

"Sure," Rush said. "But that doesn't make him my friend."

RUSH PUT on rubber gloves and got paraffin out of the gadget box. The paraffin was in a lump, and had been treated so that it was soft enough to be molded. Rush pressed it against MacCoggan's hands, then pulled it off again.

"What are you doing?" the girl asked.

"Taking his fingerprints."

"You're lying. I know how fingerprints are taken."

Rush went ahead and treated the interior of the paraffin molds with a chemical vapor, then inspected them with a complicated small magnifying glass which had near microscopic magnifying power—when he managed to make it function. He discovered numerous small greenish crystals which had formed as a result of reaction between the chemical vapor and something already on the paraffin. The discovery seemed to satisfy him.

"Hope I looked like a detective," he remarked amiably. "Particularly making those passes with the magnifying glass."

"I can't quite make you out," the girl said in an exasperated voice.

The rifle began cracking again, and its bullets broke through wood with noisy reports. In between shots, small waves rattled against the hull. Eventually the tear gas blew away, although the faint odor of it remained, a scent, somewhat like that which surrounds an overly aged egg, which was broken.

Suddenly, and for no apparent reason, Rush said, "Rory is a swing-band leader. MacCoggan is a producer of Broadway musical shows. Are there other musicians aboard?"

"Practically all of the crew are, or have been musicians," the girl said. "The steward used to pound a skin, and the engineer licked a gob stick for an early Dixieland."

Rush said, "You begin to sound a little like Rory."

The girl flushed, explained, "I mean that the steward is an ex-drummer, and the engineer played clarinet with an early jazz orchestra."

"What accounts for so many musicians?"

"Martin Dameron liked to have them around him. Whenever a musician got down and out, he could get a job with Martin Dameron. Sometimes there were dozens."

"This Martin Dameron must have been a great guy," Rush said thoughtfully.

"He was." In Sara's eyes there was abruptly a mist that did not come from tear gas. "He wasn't like you and me. He was a body and soul made out of music. He was different from other men. I think that is why his music was so incredibly moving to all who heard it. You didn't have to know music to be moved by what Martin Dameron composed."

Rush watched the girl, both because he understood what she was talking about, and because she was exceptionally easy to look at.

"His music had something that only the compositions of one or two others in the span of history have possessed," she went on. "It was like sunlight, and darkness, and something that you can feel but you can't describe."

"Amen," said MacCoggan.

MacCoggan had awakened.

RUSH VENTURED out of the cabin—the rifle had become silent—and made a survey. In order not to show his head, he used one of his gadgets, a periscope which consisted of small mirrors reflecting through a long telescoping tube somewhat thicker than a match stick. On the uppermost end of this was a stuffed sparrow which disguised the end of the lens, and by pulling a silk thread, the stuffed sparrow could be made to flap its wings, so that it was possible to give a realistic imitation of the thing flying and alighting, or hopping about. Rush was a little ashamed of this silly sparrow-periscope gimmick, and he had never let anyone see the thing.

The jungle was still and without sign of life. It was really jungle. Hurricanes had blown down trees and piled wreckage in the tangle of palms and thorn bushes. On the higher ground, a brilliant scarlet spot beyond the green of palm fronds, was a tiled roof. But not a living thing seemed to be stirring. Rush made the sparrow fly down out of sight, flapping its wings enough to get attention. Then he put his hat on the other end of the periscope tube and lifted it. The rifle cracked. The hat sailed away.

Rush went back to the cabin.

"War seems to be in prospect," he said. "Any of you know where there are any firearms? In my typical way, a gun is the one thing I forgot to include when I packed."

"I haven't got a gun," MacCoggan said. "Furthermore, I never shot a gun in my life."

"Let's you and I go prowling."

They prowled, and came back empty-handed as far as weapons were concerned, but well burdened with food, canned stuff for the most part.

Rush had thought of something to ask the girl. "How well do you know Bufa?"

She stared at him. "What?"

"Bufa. You understand—the voice of the toad."

Sara shook her head, completely puzzled, and looked at MacCoggan, who suggested, "I think he may be a little more than half crazy."

Rush said, "You wouldn't save what little sanity I have left by telling me what is behind this mess?"

For a moment, he thought they were going to give him the information, but MacCoggan shoved out his jaw and shook his head, and the girl nodded agreement.

CHAPTER V

THE MUSIC-MASTER'S WORK

AN HOUR LATER, it was dark enough.

"Now, these things are flares," Rush explained, exhibiting two shotgun-cartridge-shaped gadgets from the box. "They're small, but they give a lot of light. If anybody tries to board the boat, you use these flares. Then you give them the tear gas. I have shown you how to use the compressed-air gas grenade thrower."

"What are *you* going to do?" MacCoggan demanded.

"Just one other thing," Rush said. "Some of this new tear gas I'm leaving is doped up with a chemical that stings the skin. However, I've got a salve here that will keep it from hurting you."

"I asked what you were going to do!" MacCoggan snapped.

"This is the salve." Rush exhibited a can out of the gadget case. "Here, I'll smear it on you, MacCoggan." He busied himself, and plastered the colorless-looking paste on MacCoggan's face and hands. He got some of it on MacCoggan's clothing. He put more of the stuff on the girl.

"I asked you—"

"And I heard you, MacCoggan," Rush said. "I am going ashore to look around. You will watch the bow of the boat. Sara, here, will watch the stern, which is safer, in case they try to come aboard from the water."

"Humph!" MacCoggan said.

Rush placed MacCoggan in the bow, and left him there while he took the girl back to the stern of the boat, which was sticking out in the water. Once out of earshot of MacCoggan—if he whispered—Rush gave the girl some different instructions. He began, "Can you swim?"

"Yes. I swim."

"All right. In five minutes, I will set off a firecracker on shore. It will sound like a rifle. Instantly, you scream and fall in the water, then swim silently down the beach this way"—he showed her which direction—"for a hundred yards, then land. I will meet you there."

"Why?"

"To save your life."

She took some time to make up her mind. "I'll do it."

Rush returned to MacCoggan and whispered, "I'll be seeing you later, I hope." He dropped quietly off the bow, and instead of moving into the jungle, doubled over and moved cautiously down the beach. The day had been bright, but there were clouds now, so that the night was intensely dark.

He found the firecracker—it wasn't really a firecracker, but a noisemaker which was detonated by a mechanical device, so that it did not require lighting with a match, which was probably lucky.

It made a ripping report.

The girl screamed. There was a splash.

When Rush met her later, a hundred yards down the beach, she was panting.

"Let's get back to the yacht," Rush breathed. "I hope MacCoggan hasn't left yet."

"MacCoggan?"

"Yes. He's our polecat."

"But—"

"I know. You said that if you had a friend on the yacht, it was MacCoggan. In that case, he had you well-fooled. Because it was MacCoggan who tried to shoot you."

"How do you know he tried to shoot me?"

"You saw that paraffin I put on his hands. That was what is known to the police as a paraffin test of a man's hand to determine whether he has fired a gun recently. MacCoggan had fired one. You heard him say he had never shot a gun. He was a liar. I got to thinking. I don't believe he was on deck with the others when that hand came out of a port-hole with a gun and shot at you, after all. I think the hand was MacCoggan's."

"Then—"

"Yes, he wanted you dead, so that's why I got you off the boat with that fake rifle shot a minute ago. Let's hope he thinks you're dead. You won't be in so much danger."

Conviction came abruptly into the girl's voice. "Poor Nick and I were the only ones who knew. They killed Nick while trying to torture the information out of him. MacCoggan must have got it, or he wouldn't try to kill me."

Rush said, "I'm going to fool you and not ask what kind of information. Come on."

THE LANTERN which made light in the portion of the wavelength covered by the ultraviolet, and which was outside the sensitive zone of the eye retina, hence invisible light, was one of Rush's prides. It was as compact as a midget radio, and almost as powerful as the big ultraviolet spotlights used to secure stage effects. Like those spots, it had a lens of glass, colored black, with a carefully chosen amount of oxide of nickel. And like all strong ultraviolet spots, it caused fluorescence, or glowing, by many substances.

The paste which Rush had smeared on MacCoggan was one that was strongly fluorescent.

When Rush fanned the invisible ultraviolet beam about, MacCoggan was suddenly a faintly glowing apparition in the darkness. Rush switched the spot off quickly, lest the man notice, and thereafter used it only sparingly, barely enough to follow MacCoggan through the jungle.

MacCoggan went directly to the house. He stood on the porch and raised his voice.

"Rory!" he yelled. "The rest of you fellows! The girl is dead. You might as well come on in."

Rush, listening, felt Sara shudder beside him. She took hold of his arm, and her whisper was full of revulsion.

"None—not one of them—was loyal," she whispered. "What ungrateful wretches!"

She was slightly wrong. Three of the sailors had been loyal. At least, they were bound hand and foot and gagged. Rory and the others carried these, and dumped them on the ground.

Rory scowled at MacCoggan.

"The girl is dead," he growled. "That turns this jam session into a clambake, don't it?"

"Not necessarily," MacCoggan said. "He held up one hand with the first finger lying over the second. "You see, I've had my fingers crossed. What we all should do is come to an agreement, Rory."

"What you mean—agreement?"

"I produce the show. Rory, you direct the orchestra for the show. And the rest of you get cut in on a percentage. Say ten percent apiece on the sheet-music sales and the other royalties. Me and Rory will split the rest, on account of we furnish the brains."

Rory growled, "You think there'll be enough dough in it to make the split worthwhile to each of us?"

MacCoggan laughed harshly.

"Martin Dameron made two million dollars off the last musical show he wrote. This one is greater than any of the others. All of us who have heard parts of it know that. And this one can be ballyhooed as a newly discovered master-piece."

"What about the heirs?"

"Sara was Martin Dameron's only heir. She's dead. We can beat any other court litigation by rigging up a fake contract and forging Martin Dameron's name to it. I'll claim he contracted to write the musical comedy for me."

Rory chuckled. "It might work. I take it you know where the manuscript is hidden."

MacCoggan nodded. His face was ugly in the glare of flashlights.

"I got it from Nick before he died," he said. "It's in a secret safe here on the island. The girl knew where, but that don't matter now."

Rush, to whom it was all becoming rather clear, bent over to whisper in Sara's ear.

"All this scramble has been to get hold of a manuscript of the last musical comedy written by Martin Dameron?" he breathed.

"Yes."

MacCoggan pointed at the three bound men and said loudly, "We'll have to bump these birds. They weren't in with us, and I don't favor lettin' them in. We can ram the yacht on a reef and say they were lost at sea in a shipwreck."

Rory nodded. He was carrying a rifle. He lifted the weapon.

Rush yelled, "Hold it!"

He threw, at the same moment, a tear-gas bomb. Then he lobbed more of the bombs, as fast as he could get them out of his pockets and through the air.

When searchlight beams jumped at him, he shoved the girl behind the bloated base of a palm tree, dived back of another. He got the transparent hood out of his pocket, donned it, then twisted the black lens off the ultraviolet lantern. The lantern then spouted a blinding beam of light that had arc quality.

Rory stopped, but MacCoggan kept coming in spite of the blinding light. Rush put the lantern down, got out a bottle containing anaesthetic—he had thought he might need the stuff to overcome prisoners—and slapped MacCoggan in the face with the bottle, which broke. MacCoggan began stumbling around, gagging on the fumes.

The others were feeling the effects of the tear gas. Rush jammed his lantern so it would spout light upon them, then charged.

He hit Rory. He had not liked Rory at any time, and put all of that dislike in the swing which he landed on Rory's jaw.

He did not hit any of the others quite so hard.

SHORTLY AFTER midnight, the clouds cleared out of the sky—there had been some lightning jumping about, but that had stopped and no rain had fallen—and the moon and numberless stars spread brightness over the little tropical island.

Rush said, "I've got one gimmick left in that case of mine, and it's a portable radio. I might be able to get help with it, now that those clouds have cleared away and the lightning stopped, so that there's not too much static. But there's just one question."

"Question?" The girl looked at him curiously. "But all of them are prisoners, and I have Martin Dameron's song manuscript. What—"

"The question," Rush explained, "goes back a ways. Before this trip started, did you say anything about all of this to anyone?"

"Why, yes. I was a little worried, although I didn't know Rory and MacCoggan and the others were all crooks. But someone had tried to seize Nick, and that scared me."

"What did you do?"

"I went to a detective agency," Sara explained, "to hire a bodyguard. They told me they would have an efficient man on the yacht when it sailed, but no one showed up. I was very vexed. Particularly, since I paid the detective agency a fifty-dollar retainer. As long as they said they would have a detective on board, I don't see why they didn't keep their word—why, Rush! Why are you looking so strange?"

"I couldn't look half as queer as I feel," Rush reflected.

He asked, "Did you give the detective agency the exact course the yacht would follow?"

"Yes. They requested the information."

"When was that?"

"Day before yesterday, the day we sailed. Why?"

"Bufa," Rush said hollowly. "He couldn't get hold of me before you sailed, so he rigged it for me to overtake you."

The girl peered at him strangely. "What is this Bufa talk? It doesn't make sense to me."

Rush opened his mouth, then closed it. He saw everything now. Bufa—the unknown and undeniably fantastic-minded voice of the toad, who persisted in involving him in fantastic crimes—had for some time used detective agencies to locate unusual crimes. Bufa must have been a client of this agency, and when this girl had come to the agency with a request for a bodyguard while she went after a song, the thing had seemed unusual enough that Bufa had handed Rush the job. That a man named Nick had ostensibly hired Rush meant nothing—except that Bufa had been sly again.

"We'll skip Bufa," Rush said sourly. "I doubt if I could explain it so it would make sense."

He went down to the yacht, walking through the moonlight with Sara, and set up the portable radio. The set functioned very well. Before long, he was informed that a seaplane would soon take off from Miami to effect a rescue.

Rush was not very enthusiastic about the promptness. This was a pleasant island, and Sara was just about what he would have ordered for a sojourn on a tropical island.

But she would be nice in Miami, too.

THE GREEN BIRDS

THE FEATHERS BEGAN TO FLY WHEN CLICK RUSH LOOKED FOR THE GREEN BIRDS

CHAPTER I

LIEUTENANT JUNIFER

THE BOOK ON the care and feeding of parrots arrived in the morning's mail, which somewhat surprised Clickell Rush, because he didn't own a parrot and had no intention of acquiring one.

Rush found one half of a ten-thousand-dollar bill clipped to a page about halfway between front and back of the book.

"Oh, great grief!" he muttered.

All the rest of that day, he went around with his fingers crossed mentally, expecting the worst to happen. Nothing occurred.

Rush repeatedly inspected the wrapping in which the parrot book had arrived; there was no clue as to who had sent it.

"It's Bufa!" Rush said desperately. "It's got all the earmarks of Bufa."

Over a period of months, Rush had been doing detective work for an unusual employer, a person whose identity Rush had not been able to learn. The unknown individual, whoever he—or she—was, had from the first struck Rush as being good material for a strait-jacket. *Bufa* was the only name the unknown had given. Rush had looked the name *Bufa* up in the dictionary and discovered that it meant a species of toad that fed on slugs and snails, which was somehow significant.

Bufa was a strange enigma who was willing to put out ten-thousand-dollar fees for the solution of interesting crimes.

In his previous encounters with the fantastic, hair-raising types of mystery which Bufa was in the habit of selecting for solution, Rush had always received one half of a ten-thousand-dollar bill before the thing started, and the other half after the fireworks ceased.

By dinner time that evening, Rush was irritated at the lack of developments, and he sat and scowled at a newspaper while waiting for his steak, which explained how he happened to see and advertisement that was in the want-ad columns.

$200 REWARD—Will pay $200 for information leading to the recovery of a green parrot with yellow and red markings which gives the correct answer when asked, "How are you, Polly?"

It was a "blind" ad—no signature, and no address except a box number at the newspaper office.

"TWO HUNDRED dollars," Rush said thoughtfully.

Later his deliberations led him to go to the telephone and call a number of pet shops to ascertain the marked price of parrots, particularly green parrots with red and yellow markings; he found birds of the variety in which he was interested were the cheaper sort, and a man could take ten or fifteen dollars and pretty well have his choice.

"Two hundred dollars!" Rush said, even more profoundly.

He took a taxi down to the newspaper office, where he wrote out an advertisement of his own, and ad which read:

$1000 REWARD—I will pay $1000 for the green

parrot with red and yellow markings which knows the right answer to "How are you, Polly?"

He signed his own name and the address of his apartment.

"Be sure," he requested, "to publish the name and address on the tail end of the ad."

"You won't be bothered," the clerk said, "if you use a box here at the office."

"The reason I'm advertising," Rush said, "is to get bothered."

Feeling much better, he took a long walk in the park, although ordinarily he detested exercise. Nature had equipped him with a set of lean ropes for muscles; these seemed to need very little exercise. Rush was of average height, average weight, and an extremist in browns. The outfit in which he took the walk in the park—checked trousers, sport coat, sport shirt—was assorted shades of brown, and topped off with a brown hat that was a snappy article which a salesman had assured him one could fold up and stuff in the pocket without deleterious results. The apartment to which he eventually returned was decorated in shades of browns. Later, his doorbell began ringing.

When he opened the door, he got shoved back by a square-jawed, well-fed, smoothly dressed man who was determined.

"Breathe evenly, pal!" the man said.

The stranger made a fast circuit of bedroom, bath and kitchen. He looked into each room, found no one, seemed pleased. He planted in front of Rush, feet apart, fists on his hips, jaw out.

"Privacy will be a great help," he said.

The stranger had been carrying something in his right hand. He showed it to Rush—a detective's badge.

"I'm Lieutenant Junifer of the seventh precinct," the man advised.

"Cop, eh?"

"I'm assigned to work with the newspapers."

"Eh?"

Lieutenant Junifer took a newspaper from his pocket and held it under Rush's nose. He had pencil-ringed the advertisement which Rush had inserted.

"This aroused my curiosity."

From another pocket, he drew a second newspaper; in this one, he had ringed the advertisement offering a two-hundred-dollar reward for the parrot.

"There seems to be a hell of a strange market for parrots," he growled.

RUSH FROWNED. "Let's see if I understand. You are a police detective and you were assigned to investigate why two people should be advertising for a lost parrot. Is that it?"

"Yes."

"The story sounds strange, I must say. The police would hardly assign a cop to do something like that."

Lieutenant Junifer moved his jaw from side to side. "Don't get me wrong—the newspaper called me in. The newspapers check advertisers close, and this business of one guy advertising a two-hundred-dollar reward for a parrot, then another guy advertising a thousand-dollar reward for the same parrot, got them interested, or maybe they smelled a news story in the thing. I wouldn't know. Anyway, I've been assigned, and that's your hard luck, so don't get tough."

Rush said, "A gag."

"What?"

"I'm explaining how I got in. Two hundred dollars for a parrot!" Rush laughed and made it sound as hearty as he could. "So I thought it would be a joke if I advertised for the same parrot and raised the ante."

"You call that a joke?"

"Yep. Two hundred bucks for a parrot is a joke to begin with."

Lieutenant Junifer frowned in a dissatisfied way. "You wouldn't be chiseling?"

"How?"

"You know: Offer more money. Get the parrot. Hold up the other guy."

Rush grinned at the other man without liking and said, "If anybody is nuts enough to pay that kind of money for a parrot, would you blame me?"

"I would call you a damn crook!" Lieutenant Junifer said.

There had been up to this point considerable hardness in Lieutenant Junifer's voice, but no anger and no contempt; now both contempt and anger entered his tone.

Rush moistened his lips and his neck darkened. He sat there saying nothing while more color came into his neck and ears, then he said suddenly, "Who the hell are you to be talking like that?" He scooped up a chair.

Lieutenant Junifer sprang up in alarm, said, "What are you going to—" and did not finish, because Rush was coming toward him with the chair. Rush had the chair upraised; his tread was catlike and purposeful.

Lieutenant Junifer sprang to the door.

"A man comes here in a decent way," he said, "and by damn, you've got no call—"

The chair which Rush threw hit the door an instant after the man got outside. Rush went to the window, stood watching the street; in a few moments, he saw his visitor walk out of the apartment house and climb into a car, a long machine that had a shining, expensive look. The car drove away.

Rush went back and picked up the chair. It was awry; one of the braces between the two front legs had collapsed from the force of the impact against the door. Rush was grinning.

He told himself in a pleased voice, "Who would have thought the cops would get interested in that advertisement?... Well, heck, a man can't think of everything."

A significance that grew out of the sound of his own voice—an idea, a possibility that hit him while he was mumbling to himself—snapped the ends off his grin. Suddenly he was at the telephone.

He made three phone calls, and the final part of his conversation was the same in each instance, consisting of the four words, "No… are you sure?" the four words sounded a little more digested each time.

The police department had no Lieutenant Junifer. The newspaper had not requested anyone to investigate the reward advertisement for parrots.

Which indicated that Lieutenant Junifer might be a fake.

CHAPTER II

THE NASTY BIRD

RUSH WAS GRINNING—SOMEWHAT foolishly—when he put down the telephone. The thing had started off silly; it would get worse as it went along, he suspected.

A fog of doubt confronted him when he tried to decide what he should do next. He had made his first move—insertion of the newspaper advertisement had been a feeler, designed to learn what would happen—and he was still convinced that his unknown employer, Bufa, wanted him to become interested in parrots. Whether the parrot for which the two-hundred-dollar reward was being offered was the specific bird or not, he was not yet positive.

"Should have followed that Lieutenant Junifer," Rush grumbled.

There were a number of things he might have done, or could do next, he reflected, and not the least practical would be to catch the first train for the Canadian woods, or some such safely remote spot. If he remained, there would doubtless be complications, and before it ended, no fun at all. That is, if Bufa's previous assignments were a measuring stick.

"Ten thousand dollars," Rush said gloomily. It was a magnetic sum. Outlandish enough to compensate for the things that might happen—ten thousand dollars could compensate for a great deal.

His apartment—the living quarters part of it—was almost ordinary, but the adjacent rooms, two of them, were unusual, for these held his gadgets and the workshop in which he made the gadgets.

Rush was an inventor—an inventor with a knack, he'd discovered, for inventing things which no one else considered practical. He had perfected several hundred devices for catching criminals and been unable to unload the gadgets on any police department; in fact, his initial effort to sell the inventions to the police had resulted in newspaper publicity that insinuated he was strictly a screwball inventor, and those newspaper stories, Rush had always believed, had caused Bufa to get in touch with him.

Rush went into the workroom and began loading his clothing with gadgets just in case. Following that, he puttered around the workshop, but failed to get interest stirred, and finally ended up in the living room with his feet on the window sill and the book about parrots in hand. The book had been written by someone, he was more and more convinced as he read, who had wasted an incredible amount of time learning to what degree the emotional stability of a parrot was affected by its love life, and equally inconsequential trivia.

When a fist hammered the door—*hammered* was the word—he got up and asked, "Who's there?"

"Telegram for Mr. Rush," a voice said.

Rush grinned thinly. "That's an old one," he called through the door. "Now who the hell are you, and what do you want?"

The voice said, "Mister, are you crazy?" with such hearty disgust that Rush decided he was wrong, and opened the door.

An irritated boy in a messenger uniform stood there. He held a cage. A towel was wrapped around the cage.

"Here," said the messenger, "is your parrot. And brother, I hope you like him better than I do!"

RUSH REACHED for the cage, happened to think, "Bomb!" and gave a nervous jump. He grinned sheepishly, and explained to the messenger, who was eyeing curiously, "Get a crick in my arm when I reach for things suddenly. Old boarding house disease."

Rush carried the cage to the table, removed the towel, perceived there was a parrot inside. Mostly a green parrot; a little yellow and some red.

Rush glanced at the messenger.

"What do you mean by that crack—you hope I like him better than you do?"

"You'll find, out bud," the messenger said.

The messenger sounded so disgusted that Rush dropped the subject and turned to the parrot. "Let's see, now, what was that question?... Oh, yes—

"How are you, Polly?" he asked the bird heartily.

The parrot bristled its feathers, gave him a baleful eye, and said, "You dirty son of a skunk! You blankety blank so-and-so—" As the bird continued, its language got worse.

The messenger boy leered at Rush.

"Now you savvy what I meant," he said.

"Who gave you this piece of feathered profanity?"

"An old man."

"What did you look like?"

"Just like an old geezer. He was about as tall as you and wore a blue suit."

Rush said, "I hope I don't owe you a thousand dollars."

"Huh? The delivery fee was paid," the messenger explained, "but if you want to tip me, that would be all right. About a buck, let's say."

"We'll say two bits," Rush said. He parted with a quarter, and the messenger boy went away looking satisfied.

The parrot turned around and around in its cage, then did some ill-tempered biting at the bars, and finally hung from the little trapeze, wrong end up. An ancient, a very moth eaten bird, Rush reflected. He examined the cage and found nothing to indicate who had sent him the feathered piece of bad temper.

Rolling up his sleeves, he unhooked the cage door and reached inside. He grabbed the parrot—and the parrot grabbed *him* almost simultaneously——following which there was profanity, not all of it by the parrot. Several green feathers floated around.

There was no note: Rush looked particularly for a message-container-quill such as are fastened to carrier pigeons. Everything about the bird was standard parrot equipment.

He popped the green bird back in the cage and ran for the bathroom washbasin to wash off the blood. The feathered fiend had not bitten his finger entirely off, as he'd thought. Rush applied iodine, then beat the wall with his free fist in agony and cursed the parrot. In the midst of this angry rage, Rush gave a bark of comprehension, and dashed back to look at the towel which had been wrapped around the parrot cage. The towel bore the name of a well-known hotel, *Hacienda House.*

Rush scooped up hat, coat and parrot cage, and went down to the street, climbed into a taxicab and asked, "Know where the Hacienda House is?

"That snitzy new hotel on Central Park?"

"Yes."

I know a short cut," the taxi driver said.

When the taxicab rolled, the parrot began swearing again, using a vocabulary so profane that it was slightly embarrassing. Rush tried various methods of quieting the bird, and was squalled at.

When the cab stopped, Rush glanced up to discover they were not in the Central Park section.

"He asked, "What is this?"

"The short cut." The driver then turned around to rest the blued snout of a gun on the back of the front seat. And *this*, my friend, is the shortest cut of all." He waggled the gun to give an idea of what he meant.

CLICK RUSH MADE FOR THE WINDOW, HOLDING THE LOWER EDGES OF THE HOOD DOWN TO KEEP THE VAPOR FROM COMING UNDER.

THE PARROT suddenly approached a high point in his swearing, and Rush waited for the outbreak to subside; during this delay, a young woman came from a parked coupé where she had been waiting, opened the cab door, and got inside. She produced a small automatic which she pointed at Rush.

She told the driver, "All right, Davey. I'll take care of him."

"Drive to the boat now?" Davey asked.

"And step on it. It sails in twenty minutes."

All in all, she was a pleasant-looking girl. When she moved, it was with long-limbed grace that was agreeable.

Her eyes were rather dark and mysterious, like very distant mountains; her lips might have come from a picture; even her determination—minus the gun—would have been nice. A girl who was exquisite in a dark-haired fashion.

Rush pointed at the parrot, said, "He uses bad words."

"I know."

She was careful to hold the gun in a way that emphasized its importance.

Rush asked, "What am I supposed to do?" and grinned.

She did not return his grin, but said, "A smart man would be properly impressed that we mean business."

Davey, the chauffeur, was taking the cab rapidly downtown, keeping on water-front streets which were deserted and very rough, so that the cab rocked and jumped and rumbled and the parrot cage bounced on the floorboards, the testy inmate squalling protest.

Rush pointed at the drive and said, "Davey was planted in front of my apartment? Right?"

"All ready to follow you." The girl nodded.

"It was a lucky break for him when I got in his cab, eh?"

"Yes. I was watching your hotel, too. When you got in Davey's cab, I drove to a spot where we had agreed to meet if we got that kind of a break."

The cab stopped at a pier. There was a small and ancient steamship lying at the dock, pouring smoke from its one funnel. Obviously this tramp boat was about to sail.

"Carry the parrot—do what I say—don't argue," the girl directed in one rush.

The three of them strode out on the pier and walked up the gangplank, Davey going ahead of Rush, the girl following close behind. The girl had taken the towel off the parrot basket and was carrying it draped over her hand to conceal the automatic. When a ship's officer stopped them at the head of his gangplank, Davey produced a steamship ticket, said, "One ticket to South America. Cabin number twelve."

Cabin twelve was neither luxurious nor inviting to the eye. Scrubbing would have helped what paint there was, but mostly it needed fresh paint. And, one suspected, attention from an exterminator.

Davey shut the door, then took off his cap and produced a heavy iron bolt from another pocket and put it in the cap.

"Turn around!" the girl ordered.

Rush stared at Davey's cap and bolt—the man had made a blackjack.

"Is that really necessary?" Rush asked grimly.

"We want you to sail from South America with the parrot." Davey said. "Don't worry. I've used this homemade lullaby on guys before. Your next stop will be Buenos Aires."

"There must be a good reason for this," Rush said.

"We want you and that parrot out of the country for a while. That's all."

"Why?"

"Well… er… let's say it's so we can have peace and quiet."

Without preliminary warning, Rush looked bewildered and put up a hand to his chest. He said, "My heart! The doctor said—" in a terrible voice, then folded down, hitting the floor boards hard so that the swoon would seem genuine.

Both the girl and Davey leaped forward, the girl crying, "Quick! Lift him onto the bunk."

They picked up Rush by hand and ankles and started to move him to the bunk, but he had a sort of spasm, legs and arms, jerking furiously, and during this spasm, he managed to slap both the girl and Davey in the face. They dropped him; Rush writhed on the floor.

Davey stumbled backward until his back jarred against a bulkhead; he put his hand to his face and snarled, "He smeared something on me!" The he stared at the girl and yelled, "It's on you, too! All over your face!"

CHAPTER III

THE PARROT QUEST

THE LIQUID HAD a syrupy consistency and it had been contained in small thin-walled rubber sacs which were tied tightly at the necks with thread; Rush had held one in the palm of each hand when he managed to slap the faces of the girl and Davey, and the sacs had burst and the chemical had smeared so that they could not avoid getting the stuff on their lips, or inhaling the vapor from it.

The girl and Davey, completely surprised, did not immediately realize what might be happening; then the girl gasped and leaped to the cabin washbasin and began trying to wash the stuff off her face. She was too late. She began swaying, finally put both hands against the wall for support.

"Davey!" she cried. "Help me!"

Davey made a hoarse, savage sound and charged Rush with the drugged, stumbling awkwardness of a bear. Rush met the charge, got hold of the man's arms above the wrists. Davey was much the larger man, but the drug had taken the strength out of his muscles. Rush managed to push him back onto the bunk and the man was so weak that he was unable to get up. Rush put the girl in a chair and she remained there.

"That stuff," he told them, "will keep you woozy for about an hour."

Rush picked up the parrot cage, got hold of Davey, lifted him and half-carried, half-walked him out of the cabin—Rush closed the door behind them—and down the ship's corridors to the gangplank. Davey could walk after a fashion. He made sounds that were not intelligible. The parrot clucked angrily in the cage.

The gangplank officer stared at them.

"My friend doesn't carry his liquor too well," Rush explained.

The officer seemed dubious, so Rush flourished the parrot cage and added, "My pal had a farewell speech all prepared, so he brought his parrot along to make it, in case he couldn't."

The parrot cocked on eye at the officer and repeated some of his choicest swear words.

"Some farewell speech!" the officer said, and laughed.

Rush stumbled down the gangplank with Davey, reached the cab in which they had arrived, and put the man inside. He placed the parrot cage on the floorboards.

"Won't be gone long," he told Davey, although it was doubtful if the man could understand him.

His plan was to go back after the girl, but a man walked up to the cab and rested the snout of a gun on the edge of the opened window.

"I'm back again," the man said without humor.

Rush eyed him. "You still playing policemen?"

Lieutenant Junifer looked surprised. "You're not telling me you found out I wasn't a cop?"

"In a belated fashion."

Lieutenant Junifer craned his neck and saw the green parrot in the cage on the floorboards.

"Sam! Felix!" he yelled. "Hell, he's got the bird here! *He's got the bird!*"

Two more men came running and stared at the parrot. They were burly fellows, fair-skinned, with something definitely foreign about them, an impression that possibly came from the cut of their clothing.

"*Ja!* The bird!" one exploded, and the other said something gleeful in a foreign tongue.

Lieutenant Junifer laughed with them. They were full of joy, literally jigging with glee, as they ogled the parrot.

"Sam, you and Felix go get the girl off that boat," Lieutenant Junifer said. "We've got this thing wound up. It's all over but the slow music."

AFTER SAM and Felix walked rapidly in the direction of the tramp steamer, Lieutenant Junifer maneuvered carefully until both he and Rush were sitting in the cab. Junifer then produced two pairs of handcuffs which he tossed to Rush. "Put 'em on yourself," he ordered.

Rush donned the handcuffs, putting them on rather loose, and Lieutenant Junifer reached over and snapped them tighter.

"You know," Junifer said, "we got smart after I paid you that visit."

"In what way?"

"You raised our ante on the parrot, so we decided to watch you until you got the bird, then take it away from you. That would be cheaper than raising your thousand-buck reward."

"You the gang who advertised offering the two-hundred reward?"

"As if you didn't know!"

Rush said levelly, "There is a lot I don't know."

Junifer grinned. "Same with us. We don't know how the hell *you* got mixed up in this. We thought it was just a little affair between ourselves and Lida, Davey and Old Joe."

"Who is Lida?"

"Trying to kid me, aren't you? Lida and Davey brought you down here. We were watching your apartment and saw you come out with the parrot and get in the hack Davey was driving; then you picked up Lida and came down to the boat. We shagged along and watched. That's how come we're here."

Rush shoved his lower lip out understandingly. "That leaves Old Joe. Who's he?"

"You might as well lay off playing innocent!" Lieutenant Junifer said angrily. "Old Joe brought the parrot to your apartment. We got a gander at him just as he went in, too late to do anything about it."

"That messenger boy!"

"Old Joe—a boy? I guess he does look like one, at that. And maybe he's not over twenty. But don't let his tender years fool you."

At this point, the tramp steamer whistle gave a wheezy toot, and the vessel began backing out of the slip, convoyed by two tugs as decrepit as the ship itself.

Felix and Sam came back, Felix damning his luck in a European language.

"You didn't get her?" Junifer barked.

"*Nein.*"

"You muttonheads!"

"There was not the time," Felix explained. "Just as we get there, the gangplank she go like that." He made a "*zip-p-p*" noise and a motion with his hands.

Lieutenant Junifer gave a shrug of resignation and jerked his thumb at Rush. "You know something—our friend in brown is playing innocent."

Sam and Felix stared at Rush blankly. "How do you mean?" Felix asked.

"He claims," said Junifer, "not to know Lida, Davey or Old Joe. He claims not to have known it was us who advertised for the parrot. You'd think he was an innocent bystander."

Felix and Sam continued to stare at Rush curiously, but said nothing; finally they climbed into the taxi. They produced guns when Junifer said, "You watch him. I'll do the driving," an thereafter kept a wintry-eyed watch on Rush. Junifer handled the wheel in silence. Once, when they were stopped in traffic, he turned around and glared at Rush, said explosively, "One damn sure thing—we got to figure where you stand in this. I never made you out when I paid you that visit."

They drove west across the river into New Jersey and Rush made no outbreak while they were paying the bridge toll. The cab was an old and worn one, and like so many cabs, it pounded and rattled with wracking violence at speeds above forty miles an hour. Eventually they entered wooded hills and followed a road that was graveled, but corrugated until it was as rough as a pond surface on a windy day.

They turned off at a dilapidated rustic arch across the road. A sign—not a new sign—on the rustic arch said:

O-BAR-X DUDE RANCH
(The Wild West of Jersey)

A pair of old ruts led to a long, low cabin standing among trees. The cabin was decrepit; untrampled grass grew in front of the steps. To the left were other cabins, a row of them, most of these with shattered windows, one with a caved-in roof; in the other direction there was a replica of a Western ranch horse corral made of rails. Grass and weeds were taller in the corral than outside.

"Take them inside," Junifer ordered.

Felix cocked his revolver. "Why do that, lieutenant? They will bleed after they are shot. The mess will be easier to clean up out here."

Junifer shook his head. "We better play safe and find out who this one is." He indicated Rush. "I'll go back to town and check on him."

They tossed Rush in a room inside the cabin that was stifling with the stale air of disuse, and put Davey in another. Although Davey had recovered from the effects of the drug smeared on hi face and lips, he had not spoken. Thereafter for two hours, nothing happened.

WHEN THEY hauled Rush out of the cabin again, Lieutenant Junifer—the title seemed to be genuine, because Felix and Sam both addressed him by it at different times—had returned from the city. He wore a smirk.

"This buttinsky"—he pointed at Rush—"is called the Gadget Man. I got the low-down from the newspapers and the police. He's a private detective, and yet he ain't one, either, because he don't have a private op's license. He's an inventor who invented a lot of silly gadgets and tried to sell them to the cops, but the cops were too wise. He's got the police puzzled. He has solved some unusual crimes lately, the way the cops explained it, and they would like to know why.

"You mean," Fritz asked, "that the police do not like this man?"

"Not too much. They can't figure him. He hasn't been able to prove that anybody hires him, so they think that maybe he might be a pretty slick crook."

"Crook?" Felix widened his grin.

Lieutenant Junifer grinned back at Felix. "Which fixes it up for us."

"How does it fix it?" Sam asked.

"You ever raise chickens on the farm in the old country, Sam?"

"Never live on farm."

"Well, if you had a chicken and some varmint got it, you would naturally look around for the varmint that got the chicken. And if you saw a fox at the coop, you would just naturally presume the fox was the varmint that got your old hen, wouldn't you? Maybe you'd never look for the fox that really got the hen. See what I mean?"

Sam looked blank, said, "See? No, I don't see."

Junifer swore. "Go ahead and bop him," he growled.

Rush was standing—he was barely managing that, since his ankles were handcuffed—and before he could dodge, Sam struck him. The blow did not knock him out, but it upset him. He tried to break his fall with his handcuffed hands, succeeded partially. Sam again raised his weapon, a yard-long piece of two-by-four.

"Wait!" Junifer was dissatisfied with the first blow. He shouted, "Hell—didn't you ever knock a man out before? You'll bust his skull that way. Here, I'll show you."

Junifer grabbed the club from Sam, and Rush tried to crawl away and failed.

CHAPTER IV
DEATH IN A PRIVATE ROOM

A LONG TIME later Rush became aware that liquor smell was strong in his nostrils and the taste of it was on his lips, and he was being shaken violently, while somewhere near an orchestra with more loudness than quality was swinging out and uproar that, when one was not in the mood for music, was definitely unpleasant. Rush's head rang bell noises and his whole body seemed to go over and over in space while he tried to get his eyes open.

An open hand smashed against his face, crashed agony through his head.

"Cut it out, Tony!" a voice admonished. "There's no need of throwing your weight around."

"Damn him!" said a voice frenzied with rage. "I teach 'im! I teach 'im to have shootin' scrape in my place."

Rush got organized enough to know that he was sitting at a round table on which stood two bottles and four glasses, in a small room with was cheaply papered. The music noise penetrated through the closed door.

Of the five men in the room, four were New York State troopers. The fifth man was large, fat, dark and angry; it must have been he who slapped Rush, for now he tried again, but one of the troopers shoved him and he missed.

"Easy, Tony," advised the trooper. "Tell us how it happened."

The angry Tony said, "Four guys come in—see? About an hour ago—see? They want a private room, and I give 'em one because they're pretty well oiled."

"They were drunk?"

"Sure. But what the hell! If we turned away every guy with a snootful, there would soon be nothing' but the wolf at our doorstep." Tony suddenly grinned at his gag, which apparently had been accidental. In better spirits he added virtuously, "Better they be in here than drunken-drivin' over the highways. That's the way I figure it."

Rush, interrupting suddenly, said, "Only two of your four drunks could walk when they came in. That right, Tony?"

Tony and the policemen stared at Rush.

"They could *all* walk, far as I noticed," Tony said. "They had their arms around each other. You know—just like drunks." He pointed at Rush. "You was huggin' two of 'em."

One of the troopers asked, "And then?"

"They was in here twenty minutes, maybe, before we heard the window break and a man yell and then—"

"What did the man yell? Could you understand him?"

Tony nodded. "He yelled: 'Watch out! This damn fool has got a gun!' We understand him plain as could be."

"And then?"

Tony said excitedly, "Three shots. Bang, bang, bang! Faster you snap your fingers. After that, we bust in, and here sits this one, asleep on the table with the gun in his hand. And that one there"—Tony pointed at the other side of the table—"on the floor."

Growing suddenly chilled—his mind had not accepted the entire grisly situation until this instant—Rush gripped the edge of the table tightly with both hands, and one of the troopers seized his shoulder and tried to keep him in the chair, but Rush matched strength with the trooper and stood sufficiently erect to see over the table edge to the body that lay on the other side—Davey. It was Davey!

Davey's face was peaceful enough, but coat fabric over his chest was ragged and redly soaked.

Rush collapsed back in the chair; the sight of a body always seemed to disconnect his nervous control.

"They brought us here!" he said weakly. "They shot him. Then they put the gun in my hand."

Nothing remotely resembling belief appeared in the faces of any of the troopers. One of them made a harshly skeptical noise. "They always claim a frame-up," he said. "Looks like they would be original once in a while."

KNOWING HE was wasting time trying to argue under the circumstances, Rush heard himself producing frantic argument. He pointed at his head, gasped, "I was knocked out! You can feel the bump on my head where they smacked me!"

"If there's a bump"—the trooper nodded at the body—"that guy probably gave it to you before you shot him."

"I'm rattled," Rush thought. "I've got to get organized. This is a predicament where words won't help." He looked down and saw that he still wore his own clothes.

The police must have searched him, for his belongings lay in a small pile on the table. Billfold, wrist watch, some silver, car keys, two handkerchiefs—one from his breast pocket, the other from his trouser pocket—nothing else. Lieutenant Junifer and Sam and Felix must have removed such gadgets as they had found in his clothing.

Rush tried to stand up. They shoved him back on the chair.

"Look," he said, "if I confessed how our gang held up the bank, wouldn't that make it easier on me? Couldn't you make this second-degree murder, or something?"

"Bank!" a trooper exploded. "What bank?"

Rush took a deep breath, continued, "Here's how it was. I go into the place, see, and Spots and Muggsy stay outside in the jalopy. When I go in, I wear my handkerchief like this." He picked up the handkerchief they had taken from his breast pocket. He worked with it a moment, and it developed that the handkerchief was composed of two very thin squares sewn together on three sides to that it formed a sack. Rush pulled the handkerchief sack over his head.

"Notice how it works," he said. "I can see out, but nobody can see enough of my face to recognize it. I figured the handkerchief gag out and I'm proud of it—"

"What about the robbery?" a trooper interrupted.

"I'm comin' to that. There was only the cashier in the bank, so I points my gat at him and says, 'Lay down, you!' Well, he lays down. So then I take my necktie like this—"

Rush removed his necktie. He reached inside the tie end, pulled out the lining, a lining that was heavy gray speckled with brown and black.

The troopers stared, puzzled.

"Then I did like this," Rush explained.

He picked up one of the liquor glasses, hammered on the thick necktie lining. Instantly, there were loud reports. Explosions about like the sounds of .22 cartridges. Not one report, but hundreds of them, all occurring within the space of three or four seconds.

The stuff was a gas which had an intensely irritating effect on the eyes. In its chemical state, it impregnated the tie lining, and was released by combustion, the combustion being furnished with violence by an explosive material differing not greatly from the substance in Fourth-of-July torpedoes. Like the toy torpedoes, it could be set off by a violent blow.

Rush was moving. He had clamped both hands to his neck, holding the lower edges of the hood against the skin to keep the vapor from coming under.

He went out through the window.

Back in the roadhouse, there was a great deal of yelling, but no shooting. The gas, hurled throughout the room by the force of the small explosions, worked much more swiftly than ordinary tear gas. A pencil-type tear gas gun, Rush had long ago discovered, was effective on but one man at a time, and that only when fired directly into his face. This stuff would fill a room in hardly more time than it took a man to cough.

IT WAS near midnight when Rush walked into the lobby of the Hacienda House. He had thrown open his coat collar so that his missing necktie would not seem so conspicuous, and most of the liquor odor had evaporated from his clothing, but he was still disheveled enough to feel out of place in the lobby, which was as rich as the interior of a Castilian palace.

He went straight to the desk clerk.

"I'm in kind of a spot," he said. "I have a message for a young fellow called Old Joe, and I don't know his last name or his room number. Miss Lida gave me the message, but she didn't get to give me more information. I wonder if you can help me."

The clerk studied Rush, then turned and went to the telephone and spoke for a few moments in a voice too low for Rush to catch, then turned and asked, "What is the message about?"

"Parrots."

The clerk turned to the phone again, spoke into it, got an answer, nodded and put the instrument down. "You can go up. Room 1440."

The door of Room 1440 was open, and the messenger boy who had delivered the parrot to Rush was standing there, waiting. His eyebrows flew up and his jaw fell down when he saw Rush. Later, when Rush had approached quite close to him, the young fellow exhibited a revolver which he had been holding under his coat.

"Come in," he said dryly.

Rush entered, then nodded at the gun. "You might as well put the noise-maker away. People have been pointing them at me all evening, and none of us have gotten anywhere."

Old Joe kept the gun in his hand. "I didn't expect you," he said. "Lida and Davey were going to put you on a boat for South America with the parrot."

"Not with *the* parrot," Rush said.

"Huh?" The boy scowled. "I don't know what you're talking about."

"It figures out that there are two parrots," Rush said. "One of them is the bird you're all after. The other one is just an ordinary cussing parrot that you picked up somewhere and gave me when you saw me advertising a thousand-dollar reward for a parrot."

The boy snorted, said, "You've got a hell of an imagination!"

"The way I see it," Rush continued, "you gave me the phony parrot to throw Lieutenant Junifer and his two stooges off the trail. You wanted them to follow me to South America. You wanted to sick 'em on me, so you would be left in peace with the genuine parrot."

The boy's gun made an audible click as he cocked it. "You know a lot. Who you working for?"

"Myself."

"We figured that. You're just a smart chiseler who saw the two-hundred-dollar-reward advertisement for a parrot, so you decided there was dough in there somewhere, and decided to muscle in. So we were right about that, eh?"

"How I got involved in this is too involved to explain, right at this point," Rush said. "You might not believe me."

"Why'd you advertise, if you didn't plan to chisel?"

Rush said, "Lida is on that steamer bound for South America."

"What?" the boy exploded.

"And Davey is dead in a roadhouse up above the Bronx."

The boy began turning white.

"And I've got to clear this mess," Rush said, "or I go to the penitentiary for killing Davey."

The boy's face was paper-pale. He let down the hammer on his gun and put the weapon in his pocket. His jaw was clenched until gouts of muscle stood out in front of his ears.

"They killed Davey!" he barked suddenly. "Hell, that means they must have the right parrot!"

He whirled and ran out of the hotel room. Rush followed. The boy did not object, let Rush follow him downstairs, let Rush climb into the front seat of the roadster which was parked in the street.

"Where we headed for?" Rush asked.

"To see if they found the right parrot," the boy said grimly.

CHAPTER V
THE OTHER PARROT

BY THE TIME they had gone a block, Rush's hair began to stand on end because of the boy's driving; he sat there hoping that the first excitement would wear off the boy and he would slow his breakneck pace, but if anything the driving became worse. Rush said nervously, "Anything up to seventy miles an hour is all right with me, but the way you're driving—"

"Get out and walk if you don't like it," the boy said, and stamped the speedometer needle up another ten.

Rush tried shutting his eyes, tried staring at that stars, tried peering at his clenched hands, none of which took his mind off the wild ride.

"So there were two parrots," he said.

"Yes." The boy spoke through clenched teeth. "We hid the right one. We told Lieutenant Junifer and the others that it got out of its cage and flew away from us."

"What was the idea of that fib?"

"So they would leave us alone. I think we fooled them. At any rate, they advertised a two-hundred-dollar reward for the bird."

The roadster windows were down—it was the convertible type of car—and wind was roaring inside, boiling around. Suddenly the gale scooped off the boy's hat, snapped it back, and Rush grabbed and got hold of it while it was plastered against the rear curtain.

He saw through the rear window that a car was following them. Police! He looked more closely. Not police—police cars carried colored alarm lights, and there were none on this.

Rush turned his head to see if the boy had noticed their pursuer in the rear-view mirror. But the mirror was askew, so that it did not show what was behind them. And the boy was showing no interest in anything but speed.

With his mouth open to warn the boy, Rush changed his mind. He grinned thinly, settled back on the seat, holding the boy's hat.

If that was Lieutenant Junifer, Sam and Felix back there, let them come. It would get the whole gang together for a final roundup—

Later, the roadster lost some of its cannonball speed, veered sharply left, half-slid through a gate with inches to spare, and was in a small shipyard. They were on City Island, Rush realized—City Island, the yachting center of the New York City area.

The roadster ran out on a dock, planking rumbling like thunder under the wheels, and stopped. The boy was out instantly, running to the end of the dock and leaping onto a schooner lying there.

The schooner was about sixty feet over all, had Nova Scotia lines, appeared to be an able craft built for utility, with a minimum of brass and mahogany. There was no one on deck, and the craft was dark.

The boy produced a key and began grinding it against a padlock on the main companionway hatch slide.

"Nice boat," Rush said.

He was watching over his shoulder. He thought he saw a car stop just outside the shipyard gates, without lights, believed he discerned shadowy figures dashing through the night murk.

"Sure it's a nice boat," the boy said grimly. "We just bought her. Going to use her to go down and pick up the stuff."

Rush was looking over his shoulder. He was sure about the figures now. They were creeping out on the dock. Lieutenant Junifer and the other two. He was sure of that now.

Rush said, "Sorry, but I need that gun," and hit the boy back of the right ear with his fist. The boy was just opening the cabin slide; he sagged and would have fallen had rush not seized him. Even then, they were off balance, and half fell down the few steps of the companionway into the cabin.

Rush was feeling in pockets for the boy's gun when the lights came on and the girl, Lida, spoke angrily, saying, "Stop that and get your hands up!"

RUSH STRAIGHTENED and whirled. She was pointing a large-caliber lever-action rifle at him, and old gun that looked used and serviceable.

Rush barked, "Watch out! Junifer followed us out, and he's right behind—"

"Get your hands up!" the girl repeated angrily.

Rush glared at her inarticulately.

In the back of the cabin, there was another parrot cage, and inside it a green bird slightly marked with red and yellow, a parrot that sat calmly, undisturbed by the uproar.

Then the revolver crashed from the companionway. In the cabin confines, the report was deafening.

The girl cried out as the rifle was driven from her hands. The bullet had hit the breech mechanism.

Lieutenant Junifer came down the companion steps. He did not say anything, did not need to. Sam and Felix followed him.

Junifer scowled at the girl, said, "I thought you sailed from South America on that boat?"

"They had a radio." The girl's voice was calm enough. "I had a speedboat come out and take me off."

Felix saw the parrot, emitted a glad yell and rushed to it. Sam followed him. The two peered at the parrot. They took it out of the cage, turned it in their hands, examined it bow and stern.

"*Ja!*" Felix said. "This the bird."

"You thought the other one was the right parrot, too," Junifer said disgustedly.

"We are certain this time," Felix insisted. "This is a gentle parrot."

"Come back and watch these three you fools!" Junifer snapped.

Rush, the girl and the boy were lined up against a bulkhead. The boy was on his feet, but looked dazed.

Junifer scowled at Rush, said, "We get the breaks, don't we? How come the police turned you loose?"

"They didn't."

Junifer dropped the subject, looked around, said, "Why couldn't we use this hooker ourselves?" The idea apparently hit him as a good one. "I'm going outside and cast off and back her out," he said.

He bounded out on deck.

Sam watched the prisoners with a gun. Felix went back to the parrot, said, "How are you, Polly?"

The parrot ignored him.

"How are you, Polly?" the man repeated.

When the parrot said nothing, the man's face became a tortured mask of anxiety and perspiration came out on his forehead. He turned around and croaked, "Sam, it may be this is still not the right bird—"

The parrot spoke. It said something in a foreign language, something very fast, and totally unintelligible to Rush.

Both Sam and Felix yelled. Both with utter joy.

Rush looked at the girl and said, "This thing is utterly insane to me."

"It is a little unusual," she said.

"Mind explaining?"

"The parrot belonged to my uncle," she said. "He was a refugee from Europe. He was driven out of his native country, and he was supposed to leave without a penny, like the other refugees. But like a lot of others, he got away with a fortune. He had jewels, mostly. Nearly a million dollars' worth.

"Where does the parrot come in?"

"My uncle hired Lieutenant Junifer to smuggle him into the United States from Cuba," the girl continued. "He didn't trust Junifer, so he hid his treasure. He taught the parrot to repeat the treasure in his native language. Then he shipped the parrot to me, also sending a radio message of explanation."

Rush said, "then this parrot is a talking treasure map?"

"Yes."

"Your uncle must have been crazy."

"Not at all. He was afraid to write down the location of the treasure. Ordinarily, no one would pay any attention to what a parrot would say. And uncle had owned this parrot all his life and trained it to give certain answers to certain questions. It was perfectly logical."

Rush said, "Oh, sure," skeptically.

"Junifer killed my uncle by torture without learning where the treasure was. The parrot arrived, but we had a great deal of trouble getting it. There is a ban against parrots entering the United States, you know. Junifer found out we were trying to get the parrot, and also got a copy of the radio message which my uncle sent, explaining the importance of the parrot. Since then, Junifer has been trying to get the bird. That is what this is all about."

"Who were Davey and Old Joe?"

"My cousins. I hired them to help me."

In the aft position of the schooner, a starter gnashed steel teeth, and the motor begin firing, making a low rumble.

Rush muttered, "I figured when the thing started, it would be something crazy. It is. Bufa sure picks 'em whacky."

THE SCHOONER moved through calm water for a time, then began to roll very slightly, and small waves pounded the hull, bursting into spray that fell across the deck.

Junifer popped below decks.

"Headed her out in the Sound and lashed the wheel," he said. "She'll be all right for five minutes." He pointed to Rush. "First thing is to search that guy. He's supposed to have all kinds of tricks."

Felix did the searching, and he was thorough. He began by grabbing handfuls of Rush's shirt and tearing that garment off.

'Look here!" he exploded gleefully, and whirled Rush around to indicate the small of his back.

A small object was held to Rush's back by adhesive tape. Felix grasped it, yanked—and screamed. He shrieked again, bounced back across the cabin, wringing his hand.

Rush was moving. This, as he saw it, was his one chance. The object on his back, a hypo needle that was spring-operated, was simply a weapon that he had cached there. It was equipped to spike anyone who removed it without knowing how to do so. Eventually Felix would become unconscious, but one man out would be no great help.

Junifer had holstered his gun. Only Sam held a weapon. Rush dived for him. Sam was gaping open-mouthed at

Felix, and he was a little slow. Rush hit him. They went down. Sam's gun exploded repeatedly, driving lead into bulkheads, ceiling and floor, as they fought for it.

The girl threw herself against Junifer, wrapped her arms around him. Junifer was trying to draw his gun. He gave up the effort, struck at the girl with his fist.

The boy was running around the cabin, seeking a weapon. He finally tore the ship's clock off the bulkhead, rushed at Junifer, hit the man with the clock. The timepiece burst, wheels flew in different directions. Junifer stopped hitting the girl and fell to the floor.

Sam's gun was empty now. Rush managed to get both arms around the man, lifted him, and ran with him, crashing Sam against a bulkhead.

After that, there was stillness in the cabin, until the parrot began talking excitedly in a foreign tongue. After he had listened to the bird for a while, Rush decided it was swearing.

IT WAS four o'clock the following afternoon before the police let Rush go, and even then they were not entirely satisfied, because as Rush agreed freely, the matter was all somewhat on the fantastic side.

He was not very successful, he was afraid, in telling them that he had gotten mixed up in the parrot matter because he had been hired to do so by an individual whom he knew only as Bufa. They thought he was a liar, he could see.

The girl, however, was satisfactorily pleasant.

"We're very grateful, Old Joe and I," she said, "and we were wondering if you wouldn't like to cruise down to Cuba with us and pick up uncle's heritage."

Old Joe didn't look very enthusiastic about the idea. So Rush grinned.

"Swell," he said.

He had a suspicion it would be swell, too. He wouldn't tell anyone about it, and Bufa wouldn't know where he had gone. He would have a little peace.

He went home to pack. There was an envelope containing the other half of the ten-thousand-dollar banknote, also a note. The note was printed, read:

NICE GOING. MAYBE SOMETHING WILL
TURN UP AROUND CUBA.
BUFA.

Which moved Rush to an expression of his feelings, during the course of which he used some of the words he had learned from the phony parrot.

ABOUT THE AUTHOR

L ESTER DENT (1904–1959) was a cock-eyed wonder. Born in La Plata, Missouri, he grew up on ranches and farms throughout Wyoming, Oklahoma and Nebraska, where he experienced the waning days of the pioneer West and devoured stacks of pulp magazines. He later claimed his lonely childhood fired an imagination that went on to create concepts and characters which still reverberate in popular culture a century later.

Early in life, he knocked about various professions, was a cowboy, a sheepherder, sold shirts, and worked in a brokerage house. He briefly studied law, and almost went into banking.

Settling down in Tulsa, Oklahoma, Dent became a telegraph operator, working in the wire rooms and tiger cages of oil companies and newspapers. As a teletype maintenance man toiling for the Associated Press in the Tulsa World Building in 1928, he discovered a fellow worker writing a pulp story. When Dent learned what the pulps were paying, he decided that he was destined to be a writer. This abrupt decision was not entirely whimsical. Hs favorite author was *Black Mask's* Dashiell Hammett, and faithfully every Wednesday, he read his favorite pulp, *Argosy*. Going back to ranching days, Lester used to sneak into the cowboy's bunkhouse to devour the stacks of pulp magazines stored there for entertainment and hygienic purposes.

Dent jumped into the field during the pulp magazines' romance with Charles A. Lindbergh, the lone aviator who soloed across the Atlantic in 1927. All America had become "air-minded," so Dent's earliest yarns starred barnstorming pilots. The economy was booming. There was big money in pulp fiction.

The stock market crash of October 1929 changed all that. Pulp markets began drying up. Dent had trouble selling. He refused to give up. Branching out, he wrote detective, air-war and Western stories. Magazines folded up as fast as he could submit to them. The Roaring 20s were truly over. It was a discouraging time.

Late in 1930, with the Great Depression coming on, Lester Dent was offered a position as staff fiction writer by Dell Publications in New York. It meant abandoning a highly-paid technical career akin to being a computer technician today. But Dent yearned to see far places and do different things.

He and his wife Norma landed in the big city the first week of January, 1931. For the next five months, Lester wrote novelettes and short stories for *Sky Riders* and *Scotland Yard*, as well as radio scripts for the *Scotland Yard* radio program.

Only two years in the fiction business, his editor described Dent as "...one of the grandest purveyors of ripping, tearing, he-man action-fiction who's loomed over the magazine horizon in many a long year..." And Lester was only getting started.

When Dell abruptly folded its Depression-battered pulp line that spring, Dent discovered that the entire fiction field had gone flat. Moving back to La Plata to live with his parents, the Dents regrouped. Lester was effectively jobless in the Great Depression. Yet he still refused to surrender his dream. Having tasted the writing life, he could not return to the ordinary working world.

Gradually, Lester broke into new markets. Readers and editors alike loved his exuberant yarns spun in an infectious style. By the new year, he was back in Manhattan, grinding out pulp in all genres, often making the covers of titles like *Detective-Dragnet* and *Western Trails.* His work attracted the attention of Street & Smith, to whom Dent had sold his first four stories.

The Shadow was mesmerizing America on radio and in the pages of a new kind of pulp magazine. The company that in dime-novel days had given the world Nick Carter, Frank Merriwell and Buffalo Bill was gearing up to launch a fresh generation of paper heroes. One was to be called Doc Savage. Street & Smith thought Lester Dent would be the perfect writer to bring their Supreme Adventurer to life. He had just turned 28.

After writing a test Shadow novel, Dent began chronicling the exploits of the Man of Bronze. It was December 1932, the end of the Depression's darkest year. Simultaneously, The Lone Ranger was being created. Conan the Barbarian had just been born. Max Brand's Silvertip was debuting of Street & Smith's *Western Story Magazine.* All three heroes would go on to great multi-media fame, but none would have the lasting cultural impact of Doc Savage.

It was the beginning of the greatest creative period in the young writer's life. Over 150 electrifying Doc Savage novels would emerge from Dent's Royal typewriter, along with two dozen Doc radio scripts. Yet almost all of them appeared under a house name Lester neither devised nor desired.

Although he would go on to crack all of the most prestigious pulp markets he aimed for—*Argosy, Adventure,* and *Black Mask*—as well as slick magazines like *Colliers'* and *The Saturday Evening Post,* the career of Lester Dent as Lester Dent was drawing to a premature close. He was now and forever "Kenneth Robeson"—immortal, yet not truly himself.

When he did surface as himself, he hit home runs. Two of the most-anthologized stories ever to come out of the pages of the legendary *Black Mask* magazine were bylined Lester Dent. Featuring Miami private eye and boat owner Oscar Sail, they read like blueprints for John D. MacDonald's Travis Magee series.

Beginning in 1932 with his Lynn Lash stories, Dent also pioneered the concept of the sleuth who used tricky scientific gadget solve crimes. Other included Jee Nace, aka the Blond Adder, and Foster Fade, the Crime Spectacularist. This specialization culminated in the Doc Savage series, as well as Dent's long-running *Crime Busters* series featuring inventor Click Rush, the Gadget Man. Dentian gadgetry was subsequently appropriated by latter-day superheroes.

After World War Two, Dent found time to write mystery novels. *Dead at the Take-Off* and its sequel, *Lady to Kill,* introduced Chance Malloy in 1946. *Lady Afraid* and *Lady So Silent* exploited Dent's days knocking about the Miami sailing community, and showcased his versatility by featuring strong female protagonists. *Smith is Dead* was a forerunner to the type of crime-suspense novels he would write for the emerging paperback book industry.

After a successful 16 year run, *Doc Savage* was cancelled, along with the rest of Street & Smith's pulp chain in 1949, freeing up Lester to write whatever he chose. But the death of his parents coupled with the loss of three fingertips suffered while cutting lumber in his basement put him in no frame of mind to do any more than dabble in the emerging paperback book market.

Yet out of this period came *Cry at Dusk, Lady in Peril* and *Honey in his Mouth,* which Hard Case Crime brought out in 2009 to rave reviews, cementing Dent's reputation as top suspense writer.

For three years, Dent ran Airviews, an aerial photography service he created. It peaked with a fleet of five planes, including Dent's personal ship.

Taking over the dairy farm which had been in the family for nearly 100 years, Dent brought scientific methods to the challenges of modern farming. He is credited with being the first to bring Grade A milk into his corner of Missouri, and after decades of traveling, appeared content to live the quiet life of a gentleman farmer. He passed away at the age of 54, in 1959, just as the last surviving pulp magazines were going out of business, victims of television, the paperback revolution, and changing times.

Lester Dent died thinking his name and works belonged to a pulp past destined to be forgotten. Just a year before his passing, he scoffed at the mention of his old Doc Savage novels, saying, "They would be so outdated today that they would undoubtedly be funny. Hell, when I wrote them, an airplane that could fly 200 miles per hour was science fiction. They would be of no interest any more."

Five years after his death, Bantam Books released three Doc novels to test a market in which pulp reprints of Edgar Rice Burroughs' Tarzan of the Apes were selling briskly. Thanks in part to James Bama's powerful monochromatic covers, Doc Savage sales surged and surged until millions of copies were sold, making "Kenneth Robeson" one of the best-selling authors of the 1960s—a posthumous vindication which, for all his imaginative powers, Lester Dent himself never envisioned.

Dent has been called the Father of the Modern Super-hero, and with good reason. As the co-creator the perennially popular Doc Savage, he laid the foundation for generations of superheroes to come. Superman owes much of his mythos, as well as his Fortress of Solitude, to the Man of Bronze. Batman borrowed his scientific training and utility belt filled with ingenious gadgets. The format of the Doc Savage series was a major inspiration for Stan Lee and Jack Kirby's ground-breaking Fantastic Four, which spawned the Marvel Universe. The creators of landmark series ranging from The Man from U.N.C.L.E. to The Destroyer have acknowledged the Doc Savage influence.

One can trace the roots of heroes as diverse as *Star Trek's* Mr. Spock and *The X-Men's* Beast back to the pages of *Doc Savage Magazine.* And James Bond's world-famous cinematic gadgets owe more to the inventive genius of "Kenneth Robeson" than they do to Ian Fleming. And what are Clive Cussler's Dirt Pitt and Buckaroo Banzai but updatings of the Man of Bronze?

Sixty years after he left us, Lester Dent's works remain in print, lost stories continue to trickle out, and his rich legacy continues to grow.